The Man From Armagh

To Peter,
in acknowledgement &
appreciation of a
friendship that has
spanned seventy years,
enduring, steadfast &
dear for each & every
day. Proud to have
been your friend.
Bob Davidson

THE MAN FROM ARMAGH

The collapse of Saint Ethelburga's medieval church, triggered by the IRA "Bishops Gate" truck bombing of April 1993

CITY OF LONDON POLICE PHOTOS

The Man from Armagh

The Sequel to The Tuzla Run

By Robert Davidson

First Print Edition

ISBN: 9781092496834

The Man from Armagh

©2019 by Robert Davidson

All rights reserved

This book is a work of fiction. People, places, events, and situations are the product of the author's imagination. Any resemblance to actual persons, living or dead, or historical events, is purely coincidental

Ocean Highway Books

For Wendy

Whose belief and support make it possible

Prologue

Spider exhaled the smoke from the Monte Cristo, one of his few vices, and watched as it spiralled lazily upwards towards the ceiling of the veranda. He brought the cigar up to his lips and blew softly on the ash, not enough to cause it to drop but enough to invigorate the red glow. Reaching for the decanter on the small table beside his wicker chair he poured a measure of Glayva, Rath's favourite tipple, into the Glencairn glasses. This one glass would be his sole intake of alcohol and only on those evenings Rath came to socialize.

He shifted in his seat and moved his feet off the footstool to relieve the ache in his knees. Any spell longer than ten minutes in one position fossilised his joints. He sighed.

It was always about this time, when the sun was setting on the yard arm that Rath would come by. Mostly they would sit in long spells of companionable silence and any conversation would be minimal. Together they would contemplate the glorious blaze of vivid orange and gold that would succumb all too quickly to the encroaching darkness pushing the sun below the horizon.

A colourful patina of artificiality came with dusk in this part of the world, but it didn't detract from the raw beauty of the sea and sky. The rapid loss of daylight morphed the palms, at the edge of the sand, and rocks standing in the shallows into silhouettes. *Like a theatrical backdrop for South Pacific. Why that musical when I'm sitting on decking in Manatee County, Florida? Age, I suppose.*

He sipped the drink then gave a start as he realised Declan was seated on the other side of the table. His friend grinned at his surprised reaction. Spider shook his head.

'You'll give me a heart attack one of these nights. I wish you would stop doing that.'

Rath did not reply but continued to smile. He'd stopped smoking around the last time he was in the Bogside all those years ago, but Spider was sure he still liked to see someone else enjoy the pleasure of a good cigar. He never asked if the aroma disturbed him; just accepted that it was at least tolerable out of doors.

Sometime later he looked over at Rath who seemed particularly meditative. Looking at his profile it continually caused him amazement that Declan never seemed to age.

"You're like Dorian Gray,' he mocked good naturedly. Rath looked across and shrugged but his eyes twinkled.

They never talked much about what had happened in the past but remained content to sit together while each looked back to those earlier times of shared actions and locales that were to populate their memories.

Once they had fought on opposite sides. They had tried to kill each other on the steps of Queen's University when Rath was an IRA soldier and Spider in the SAS. Both were wounded in that fracas which turned out to be costly for both.

They would meet up again in another war, in Bosnia, where paradoxically they would face a common enemy together as they drove convoys through the Serbian lines to Sarajevo, Zenica and to other cities and towns. That fateful run to Tuzla had been the catalyst that changed everything.

The experience would forge a friendship that was as lasting and meaningful as it was unlikely.

Chapter One

Liam stared, without expression or emotion, into the pale wood coffin on the makeshift bier formed by Ma's front room table. He did not recognise her. His first thought was, 'This is not my mother.'

The casket was open, revealing head and shoulders. Her skin looked waxen and jaundiced despite the light covering of face powder. Pronounced wrinkles made the contours of her careworn face sag. She looked much older than her sixty years. He did not remember her ever looking young. Nor smiling.

The agony of the sarcoma had ravaged her features and even in death, the pain she suffered was evident. He sniffed, then grimaced. The cloying scent of cheap supermarket hair spray used to complete her post-mortem set hung in the air.

There was no sense of loss at her passing. Never close to any of his kinfolk he did not give a moment's charitable thought to his mother. She had receded into the grey group of shadows who meant nothing. His mother's inability to intercede on his behalf in his early years and protect him from his father's violence had rankled when he was still at the age when he had sensitivities. Then, in the process of time, hardened like fists pickled in brine, his finer feelings solidified into indifference.

This apathy applied to all others including his sibling. His birth had brought no joy nor happiness

in the gaining of a brother. He experienced neither envy nor sadness in losing his place as the only child.

This brother engendered no solace, no fraternal bonding, as he turned out to be a weak mewler. Not once had he uttered the boy's name. Never voiced it, ever. Like Bill Sykes, who had given his dog a name then never used it. He was not sure if he even thought of it when the boy crossed his mind. Liam had tormented him without mercy and the other's pain had given him a perverse pleasure. As a youth he had experienced highs at the screams of agony. His younger brother's feet and lower legs had ugly scars where the ignited lighter fluid had melded the ashes of his socks to his skin. The knowledge that this victim was *his* brother, that the boy would weep and beg for him to stop, was somehow comforting to him. This proprietary sense was the nearest he could come to fraternal affection. They shared an experience; he in administering the torment and the younger brother suffering its hurt. Liam could not display or feel love or compassion.

They were nonentities, she and the brat. There was no valid place for either. As they were without value in his life there could be no emptiness, sadness or ache of any kind. The boy lacked backbone, spunk, testosterone or whatever. How he had been killed in Croatia, of all places, belied creditability. And yet— he had been his brother.

But the killing at another's hands?

That was something else entirely. This reeked of challenge. It was an affront. It caused umbrage. More so, if the members of the organisation to which he belonged had colluded to bring it about. The boy's demise in Croatia needed explanation considering the rumours that his death had been ordered by the leadership of the IRA.

Now they were no more. Gone. Each one. And soon, with the recurrent and relentless progression of the cancer, his life too, would end.

He recalled the earliest of his frequent beatings that occurred when, as a five-year-old, he tried to protect his Mammy. Filled with abject terror, screaming with pain and shocked at this first brutal betrayal by his Daddy, his breath strangled by the tears and the snot lathering his face he begged for it to stop, even when it had. His father a frustrated, weak willed man had been all too aware of his own shortcomings which copious amounts of Guinness and Maundy's failed to dispel. The alcohol instead torched and stoked the brutish disposition lying just below the surface His first born suffered the brunt of his inadequacies. The violence of the whippings hardened Liam and, as the thrashings increased in severity, he grew, becoming resilient and resolute in the face of it all. He smiled without humour as he recalled the times bigger youths would beat him up, often in twos or threes, and through bruised and broken lips, he would infuriate them by mocking their efforts to subdue him. *Is that the best you can do?* He acquired a capacity to withstand pain and his ability to suck it all up increased as his body grew in strength.

The son of a Catholic father and Protestant mother he needed to be hardy. Neither faith would accept him. The neighbours' distrust and dislike spawned the cruelty that infected their offspring who then bullied him without mercy as only children can. To be of mixed-race in the North attracted snide comment but mixed religion was a universal anathema. The family moved twice to start afresh when it became known in the street that a Taig and a Prod shared the same bed.

He could not remember what made him a loner or when he became one. His father no longer constituted a threat and had long since ceased to impact on his life. The final time his father tried to alleviate his frustrations by whipping him he reversed the roles by beating the man senseless. He couldn't decide if the ensuing exhilaration came from subjugating the Alpha male or from the recognition that their pack had a new top dog, or a compound of both.

As he developed, taller and stronger, the number of beatings did not diminish, but now, he administered them to his former tormentors and others. The experience of the erstwhile beatings did not make him charitable; it prompted him to adopt his former oppressors' attitudes to cruelty in such a way it became *his* hallmark. Those who lived in dread of his attention called him Genghis. He gloried in the name.

His father died on his fourteenth birthday. He frowned. *It's a struggle to remember what the man looked like.* A raging sot long before Liam's birth, he'd drunk himself to death at a relatively young age, even for that part of the world. Liam detested his father still, with an unabated intensity that he nurtured. He did not grieve or have a sense of loss over his parent's demise and refused all his Mother's entreaties to go to the funeral. *Why should I go? I spent every waking minute of my childhood wishing the bastard dead! It wasn't as though I needed proof!*

He became an enigma relying on his wits, strength and abilities to survive but aware of the value of alliances. He accepted that a team, led and made cohesive by a strong leader, achieves more than an individual. Soon, he had formed his own gang of youths ruled by the power of his fists and he directed their efforts in several nefarious projects. With no real interest in the illicit gains, he doled out much of his share as incentive to the members for their loyalty. Success continued for two or three years; they robbed small convenience stores, effected burglaries, and implemented protection rackets. Until the day they inadvertently mugged and robbed a drunken Ulster Defence Force man, relieving him of £600, his winnings from four hours in the local bookie's. This became a pivotal moment in Liam's life. The man's older brother was an inspector in the Royal Ulster Constabulary. Liam would appear on the law's radar for one of the few times in his life.

Chapter Two

The green, unmarked van halted at the gate and the armed guard, covered by the weapons of two others, checked the I.D. and documentation of the driver and escorts. The officer behind the wheel handed over the prisoner manifest, together with the photographic head shots, and they were compared against the occupants of the vehicle. Liam had the good fortune to be classified a youth —two days short of his eighteenth birthday—and was to serve his sentence as a juvenile. The prisoner handcuffed to him would serve his sentence as an adult.

As the vehicle pulled forward into the main compound a heavy drizzle began. A guard ordered the detainees to get out and line up in single file.

HMP Magilligan, County Londonderry, was to be Liam's home for the next eighteen months. Eight Nissan huts formed the prison, which had opened a few years earlier. It had been an army camp, but the military had moved to Shackleton Camp leaving its accommodation to house the various paramilitary miscreants undergoing confinement at Her Majesty's pleasure. Later, other prisoners convicted of non-terrorist offences, and Borstal trainees, would also serve their sentences there.

Within the first week of his detention Liam realised the authorities, the Warden and warders, did not wield the power in the prison, but the disciplined ranks of the illegal militias held sway. The paramilitaries belonged to powerful organisations on the outside. The threat and menace behind the phrase, 'We know where you live,' was blatant. All the Government employees feared the implications and the hazards knowing how vulnerable their families were to the dangers.

Each day the factions held their own parades in the exercise areas, practised drilling, counter marching and fitness training. They also had their own instructors for their doctrinal and educational needs.

Liam was under no delusion that time off for good behaviour would play any part in his enforced sojourn here. To conform for the sake of convention had no place in his makeup. He saw a way to gain from this confinement and would use it as an opportunity for self-improvement, recognising knowledge was power, and education the key.

He had no problem with the political factions, who considered themselves a class apart. They remained aloof from the bickering and bullying that persisted among those they categorised as 'petty criminals.' This suited him well enough, but if the IRA or, less likely, the Protestant paramilitaries, asked him to join he stood ready. To look a gift horse in the mouth had never been one of his failings. There was a new prison under construction on the disused airfield, close to Maze racecourse, near Lisburn, and the Politicals would eventually move there.

He did not doubt for one moment, when the time was right, an organisation would offer him membership and he would accept. Recruitment was a thriving activity behind the wall. To survive, one had to be part of a group. A man couldn't watch his own back twenty-four hours a day. Although, he was not a follower for the sake of being a member of a community, he had always recognised the advantages of group strength and leverage.

To get the Republicans to notice him, he would engineer an invitation but with finesse and under his own conditions. It wouldn't do to join a system as an insignificant cog at the lowest level of *their* machine.

Three weeks of his eighteen months' sentence elapsed. The time had been problem free, or at least nothing insurmountable. He kept his head down remaining uninvolved. This was not acceptable to everyone in Magilligan. A brute of a youth, Slab Ritchie, sentenced for robbery and four cases of grievous bodily harm, GBH in officialise and prison parlance, together with his crew, was becoming irksome. They had already subjected two teenagers, admitted on the same day he arrived, to the conventional prison application of control by abuse; pain, rape and humiliation.

Ritchie broadcast to all and sundry that Liam was high on his list for attention. While Slab's two cohorts held him face down over a sink in the ablutions, Richie told Liam, in explicit detail, what he could expect. It would be crude and unpleasant but he, Slab, would decide where and when it would happen. His interest in Liam was specific. His uncle, the UDF hero, mugged and beaten, was the reason for MacDermot's presence in Magilligan. After slapping him several times, he grabbed him by the crotch. Then running his tongue over his lips to make a wet moue he mouthed Liam's eyes shut before slamming his fist into the other inmate's lower abdomen. With a signal from him the two handlers let go. Liam dropped, and all three took a kick at his prone body, one boot contacting, with a sickening squelch, the base of his skull.

◆◆◆

After twelve days in the sick bay Liam returned to the prison's population. Unsurprised that no investigation into the attack had taken place, he showed no dismay. He would himself administer the castigating action.

The rain, substantial drizzle which, propelled in sheets across Lough Foyle and the open headland to slash at the panes of reinforced glass, darkened his mood. The dank weather of autumn and winter always affected his spirits. More morose than usual and subject to extreme anger—not blinding, storming furies but cold, clinical rage that honed his violence he felt the internal pressure increasing. Dispassionate, cold in relation to others he was slow to anger until they vexed him — he could then hate and apply it with savage vehemence. Control was never a problem and he would give in to the desire to destroy only when he decided.

He put down the tattered copy of Life magazine to stare at the wall. The strength and aptness of the phrase he had just read resonated. While never able to verbally express it so concisely, it had been his credo over the years and had stood him in good stead in many physical confrontations. He loved the power implied by the term.

Slab Ritchie's attempt to intimidate him, using lewd sexual threats and obscene narrative, was laughable. But it would stop. Dead. Nipped in the bud. To achieve standing in the prison population and survive Magilligan, there was no alternative. Ritchie was 'connected' with big guns in the Protestant paramilitary on the outside, but this would not be detrimental to Liam's bid for recognition. Just the reverse.

It would happen soon.
In fact, why not now?
He rose and removed the rolled socks from his footlocker, separated the pair and held one open to drop in the unused brick of hard industrial soap. Applying a knot just above the block he gripped it by

the leg before hefting it in his hand and slamming it into the metal door of his locker, causing a substantial dent to appear. Satisfied, he put it in his pocket allowing the leg to poke out and in easy reach of his right hand. He picked up the opened publication, re-read the caption and mouthed the phrase that fired his imagination.

The Pre-emptive Strike.

◆◆◆

Slab Ritchie and one of his acolytes, Crewdson, were playing snooker while Devlin, the second minion, watched from the sofa against the wall of the recreation room. Ritchie, stretched over the table to sight along his cue, looked up and smirked as Liam entered. There were three other inmates playing cribbage near the window. Liam noted that one was Ciarán McCormack, who was head of the IRA hierarchy in the institution.

'Here's ma wee puppy, looking for a shag and about to get a face full of ma dick,' Ritchie snorted derisively. Crewdson guffawed.

'Are ye ready for a good beasting, ye feckin' pansy?' Slab asked, as he missed sinking the blue.

Liam, with his back to the second unoccupied table, said nothing. He pulled the sock clear of his pocket and twisted the leg around his hand moving to stand between Devlin and Ritchie.

The unsuspecting Devlin gave a high-pitched scream as the block of soap connected with his left eye socket. Both hands flew to his face and he fell forward onto his knees whimpering. Crewdson, whose turn it was to play, half turned, still leaning over the table, as the home-made mace pulped his cheekbone and jawbone with a sickening crunch. Blood gushed from his nose to pool on the green baize.

Ritchie countered his shock by trying to flee the room but to get to the door he had to run past Liam, who tripped him with a full leg sweep. As he fell, the loaded sock mashed his collar bone and shoulder. He dropped his cue. Holding his damaged shoulder, he cringed as Liam placed a foot on his back forcing him to remain on the floor. He attempted to twist away from the hand on the waistband of his tracksuit bottoms. The sock-covered soap thudded into the right-side of his face and, semi-conscious, he was helpless. Liam ripped his trousers down. Slab shrieked with ear-piercing intensity as the point of the cue ripped through his underpants and rammed into his anus. He was oblivious to the fresh pain when Liam forced his right hand onto the edge of the table and crushed his fingers with the overworked blood-sodden cosh.

◆◆◆

With the removal of Ritchie and his entourage to the A&E at Atnagelvin hospital no one seemed prepared to fill the vacuum created by their absence. The injured youths adhered to the code of silence and did not implicate Liam, although he suspected that this was not voluntary but prompted by 'guidance' provided by McCormack. The specific incident did not affect the hard men, but the practice of informing was abhorrent. They would involve themselves in the prevention, with violence, of any breaches.

Despite this, Liam entered solitary confinement, but the Warden released him, after three days. There was no evidence or witnesses. The assault would go unpunished.

Liam showed no surprise when three Republicans, one of them McCormack, stood with their trays until the others at his table looked up, then in haste gathered their plates and cutlery and scurried away. A silence ensued that Liam determined not to break.

McCormack's two companions chewed stolidly as he addressed Liam.

'You'll be considering yourself untouchable now you've educated Slab and his boys?'

'No.'

'Then you're not stupid. That would be short-sighted and you're not that. Have you thought of joining?'

Liam thought to play naive by pretending not to understand the question, but his feral intuition made him think better of it, though he still lied, 'No.'

'Give it some thought.'

The conversation lapsed, as they concentrated on the food before them, the quality of which did not warrant such attention.

Liam became a member of the IRA while in Magilligan but, for reasons of his own, convinced

McCormack it could be to the organization's benefit were he not identified as one. Ciarán, who was several years older than Liam, knew from experience that being a known IRA member and yet attempting to deny it when challenged, was not always ideal and had its downside. The advantage was that Liam would not transfer, before his release, with the Politicals to Long Kesh. When the time came, he could join a unit on the outside with little fanfare.

He participated in the various extra mural and educational activities organised by Ciarán. He made a good impression on those who had influence in the organisation. However, as time passed, slow and without momentum, the triviality of life behind bars became pointless and tedious.

Although no one publicised his allegiance and membership of the behind-the-walls Republican Army, the warders had taken note of who he associated with and he found himself excused from the normal, boring, down-and-dirty jobs assigned to the others. With no knowledge of the post or previous experience in a like position, he worked in the library as assistant to one of Ciarán's deputies. The job gave him access to the books and magazines he would not otherwise have seen. As his threshold for boredom was low the wealth of literature available helped to assuage the ennui and the approach of his discharge came almost as a surprise. With only two more weeks to endure Magilligan he became restless and eager to leave. He was sweeping out the library when he looked up to see Ciarán at the counter. The older man beckoned him.

'Another thirteen days?'

'Yep, and not too soon.'

'Nothing special lined up, have you?'

'I wish. No, just back home and into the usual day-to-day rubbish.'

'In that case, we have something for you. A chance to develop and to help where it's needed. But, listen, this'll be the opportunity of a lifetime— your opportunity to do something positive for us.'

Ciarán held Liam's gaze then leaned forward to continue.

At times thinking caused the aches to intensify. Even the recall of memories was an effort causing strain he tried to avoid.

Rubbing the back of his neck to relieve the headache coming on he remembered that he had not taken his medication. From the cupboard above the sink he took down a mug and filled it with water. As he swallowed the tablets, his eye caught sight of the Coronation biscuit tin on the bottom shelf. His mother used to keep all the official notifications and bills, in that container. The family received correspondence but never letters. Who would write? Liam took the tin to the front room and sat down in the battered wing chair before the empty hearth. The formal letter from Geneva, identified by the Suisse stamp, was on top of the hodgepodge of assorted forms and faded box Brownie photos. He put on his glasses to read. After returning it to the envelope, he leant his head on the backrest and stared at the grey ceiling.

His brother had died in Bosnia, in a vehicle accident, from injuries sustained, the letter claimed. This he would have accepted had it not been for other knowledge coming to light before this written confirmation.

When he had first learnt that the mewler was a driver for the commander of the East Belfast Battalion, he laughed at the incongruous image. That snivelling git serving as a volunteer?

Later, on hearing his younger brother was often a member of an ASU with a credible success record, he was more sceptical. Active Service Units, used for offensive hands-on ops were, wherever possible, staffed only with members with bottle. The revelation he was the source of information passed to the British about the Queens University operation was not a surprise. After an initial grilling by the Nutting Squad Calum had gone to ground. This forestalled a second grilling by Cosoleto's interrogators. Sean Diffin sent the Removal Man to find him. The hitman's remit was never made clear by Diffin, but Calum did die after Declan Rath met up with him. Rath's role had always been eliminations. From sources in the IRA, who denied the object was to kill Calum, he learned that Rath and Calum were on the University operation together and much later, from another informant, he discovered Calum had rescued the wounded hitman. This alone made the report of Calum's treachery less than convincing for him but did not, illogically, affect his growing belief that Rath killed his brother.

He regarded this version of the whole episode as contrived, intended as a deliberate affront to him and, more so, to degrade his reputation and reduce his standing among those on the Army Council. Their prior determination, Diffin's and his sycophantic guppies on the Council, to hide from him his brother's alleged disloyalty had been to ensure he would have no input on its resolution. All of which had constituted, in his mind, an ulterior motive to discredit him and his earnest belief that peace negotiations were a surrender of the basest order. To him it was evident that only aggression exercised with unremitting violence would win the day. Dislike, hate, of Sean Diffin, the current Chief of Staff, influenced his thinking more than any regard for what had happened to his brother. But he never allowed analysis of his emotions to challenge or influence his gut feelings.

In his eyes Diffin was everything he wasn't; he was IRA aristocracy if not royalty. *A scion of a fucking dynasty.* His forebears had been active in the Irish Republican Brotherhood on both sides of his family; his great grandfather died in a bungled bomb attack in the bombing campaign in England in 1868. A grandfather fought in the Irish War of Independence and his father had been shot by the RUC during an abortive attack on one of their stations.

Sean had also experienced action but only as a patsy on the sharp end of it, when he took three bullets from a Loyalist murder crew. He survived the failed assassination attempt because of the weak penetration capacity of the bullets used. Liam believed the authorities, forewarned about the impending assassination attempt, replaced the ammunition in the Loyalist cache with low velocity ammo. Why?

After that it was the sunny side of the street for the high and mighty Diffin, waltzing along and upwards in the ranks of Sinn Fein. True, he served time in Long Kesh and 'master-minded' a breakout but Liam continued to doubt the veracity of any of Diffin's glorified saga and saw it all as posturing. Any breakout from a high security institution was impossible without connivance from the staff. Some of them *could* have succumbed to threats and colluded but perhaps the complicity was authorised, and the escape contrived as a stage in developing the cover story a well-placed informer would need?

While Diffin was rocketing his way upwards through the ranks of the political 'warriors' Liam was soldiering in the true sense of the word. It never sat easy with him that there were so many anomalies in Diffin's life that only he and no one else could see.

Diffin had been covertly released from prison by the British to attend secret negotiations held in London while he was still a low-level representative of the movement. That it was a prerequisite of the IRA's participation raised another question. Whose condition was it? Why would the Council want him there? Was the stipulation proposed by the British or, more likely, on their behalf by another stooge of the British inside the organisation?

The authorities had overwhelming evidence, statements from turncoats and their own tribe of measly informers that Diffin was high ranking IRA but he never faced prosecution. Even the papers published theories that implied conspiracy.

These developments occurred while creating a legend to protect the highest ranking supergrass of the British. They had gone to extraordinary lengths to build a front for him and craft a reputation for him to hoodwink the rank-and-file members.

Then there was Brendan Diffin, the kiddie fucker. If they knew about *his* predilections, then that would be another string to their bow in coercing compliance. The younger Diffin had been a close friend of that other molester Father Brendan Smythe who was holed up in some monastery in Eire. The mole in the RUC assured him that MI5 had chapter and verse. So, had they put that to use or not? He snorted in humourless laughter.

He rose from the chair and filled the kettle in the kitchen. As he leaned against the sink listening to the water boil, he nodded to himself,

'Yes, Sean you bastard, you're going down and it won't be to prison. You'll be experiencing, not the British Justice system, but mine.' That he could not prove any of his suspicions would be no bar to the action he would take. The IRA's evidentiary policy was to err on the side of security. If there were suspicions of treachery, then that doubt alone was enough for summary judgement and for sentence to be carried out.

Liam MacDermot would be judge and executioner.

The painkillers slowly kicked in. As he relaxed, his thoughts drifted back, over the chasm of dead time, to his release from Magilligan

Chapter Three

Seated behind the driver, he watched the rain as it rattled against the windscreen in a continuous litany, interspersed by the screech of the wipers, as they tried, with little success, to hold the deluge at bay. 'Bloody July!' A sullen and disgruntled Liam could smell the damp as it evaporated from his second-hand tweed jacket. Released two days ago, his first upset, when about to return to the free world, was that his belongings had been 'mislaid' by the quartermaster staff. He had made his feelings known, in no uncertain terms. The civilian clothes, without doubt those of a homeless dosser sentenced for vagrancy, lay on the counter before him. The warder on duty offered, with a sneer, to process the paperwork to buy new shop-bought garments. The downside would be deferral, by a week or three, of his release date. Liam buckled and grudgingly accepted the apparel. His next let-down was when he discovered that his mother had altered all his clothing at home as hand me downs for his gobshite of a younger brother.

Frustration followed frustration in the screwed-up process of trying to get to his destination in the Republic. Within minutes of leaving Belfast he was in countryside that had to be thirty years in the past. And he was still in the North! And in rural Eire, you could add another ten years to the previous time zone of past existence.

Unaware that the bus had stopped to pick up passengers until blasts of cold air from the open doors enveloped him, he watched as a woman with a pushchair and three young children stepped forward. She heaved the first into the bus then looked at the driver and Liam, for help. Both remained seated and the driver looked away. Liam stared past her at the expanse of turf and bog stretching to the base of the mountain mass in the middle distance. Utter bloody desolation. A thought struck him, and he screwed around in his seat to take in a three-hundred-and-sixty-degree scan of the land. Not a house in sight. Just an emptiness all round. No trees, no houses, not even telegraph poles.

With no other thoughts to occupy him he spent the rest of journey to Mullaghmore puzzling the answer to the bedevilling poser.

'Where in the hell had they come from?'

◆◆◆

Liam looked up from the newspaper noting the two newcomers but returned his gaze to the print before they looked in his direction. Head down over the opened pages, with the glass of Guinness on the top right corner of the right-hand page, as instructed by McCormack, he sensed someone approach. He looked up to see the taller of the two, while the dark-haired one remained at the bar.

'Would you be having another?'

Liam raised his glass, with his left hand, again as stipulated by his former mentor, and drained it.

'Aye, I would,' he replied without a smile and took one of the filled glasses from the offeror. He watched as the man pulled out a chair and sat across from him.

'Coyne. Thomas.'

'MacDermot. Liam.'

'Who?'

'McCormack,' responded Liam completing the final part of the check. Coyne relaxed and made a hand motion towards the bar. His companion, glass in hand, came over and taking a chair, joined them, adjusting his position to avoid the sun's rays coming through the window behind Liam.

'This is Frank Dooley.' They nodded to each other but made no overtures for a full minute, then Coyne asked,

'How did you get acquainted with Ciarán?'

'We shared at Magilligan and he mentored me. He taught me how things are and briefed me on what I was to do on release. Here I am.'

Coyne stood and came around the table to sit beside Liam, causing him to slide along the bench.

'Despite you being a novice, you're now part of the team. I'm to be in charge of your training.'

'That much they said, but not what sort of training.'

Coyne swallowed a draught of the dark liquid and took a long slow look around the bar.

'I'll tell you soon enough. Can you drive, boyo?' MacDermot nodded and toyed with the glass in front of him.

'Where are you staying?'

'Here.' Liam showed with a nod he had a room above the bar. 'They sent a package for you.'

'We'll want you out of here, but no rush. Time enough for the packet later. We'll just finish these, maybe one more, and then we'll get started,' said Coyne, in no hurry to move.

◆◆◆

On the third day Liam transferred his sparse belongings from the bar to a small room in Coyne's cottage. There appeared to be no urgency to start his training and they spent most of the time just talking. Liam guessed they were putting him through a test, but their approach seemed so laid back, almost lackadaisical, that he couldn't fathom what they were trying to discover. In fact, he thought he now knew more about them than they did about him.

During the long sessions of conversation, he learned that Coyne had served in the British Army at one stage and had training, first as an ammunition examiner and later as a bomb disposal technician, at a place called Bramley, somewhere in the backwoods of southern England.

For the next two weeks his training continued at a leisurely pace and to Liam's mind, was half-hearted and with no sense of purpose. Dooley gave some rudimentary instruction in the taking apart and re-assembly of an AK47 that had seen better days. Liam had never fired a weapon and got no clue when he might. He became familiar with the Browning pistol, a battered Garand rifle and heard about the recent acquisition of Armalites from the States although they left him in no doubt, that *he* wouldn't be using one of those for a long time.

In answer to his questions about his part in any actions Coyne was uncooperative and crude in his snarled responses and irritated Liam by repeatedly addressing him as 'Boyo'.

The older man, Dooley, briefed him about members of the local Gardaí and their appointed beat times. He pushed him with rigour on the training runs with the Land Rover and concentrated on instilling a sense of urgency into Liam. The youth drove fast but without recklessness. As the halcyon days of that July were elapsing, Liam developed an intense dislike of the cell leader Coyne but never allowed this to show. This was one of his strengths-- the ability to keep his emotions under the radar. But there would come a time when he would avenge himself on the bomb maker. Liam believed revenge was a dish best served cold and force-fed.

Where there was no latitude, flexibility or *laissez faire* was in the assembly sessions of the explosive devices, which were long and detailed.

Aspects of the process caused him to silently applaud the ingenuity that had created the most effective and deadly tools used in the war against the British. Coyne told him of the early days when the Army shot youths supporting the cause before they could throw their petrol bombs, because of difficulty in lighting the fuses on windy streets. Now, strips of newspaper, soaked in sodium chlorate then dried, and tied around the bottles would ignite the petrol when the glass broke, as the gasoline re-acted with the chemical in the paper, obviating the need for lighting. It was clear to Liam that the IRA's ability to improvise and improve their weaponry had started with small steps but was now in its stride.

Coyne was proficient and knowledgeable on the whole range of material for bomb making; detonators, timers and remote-control components, all stored under the garage. The bombs themselves appeared rudimentary in composition and basic in the materials used to complete them but were no less dangerous for that.

'Put them latex gloves on. This stuff can give you headaches worse than a hangover 'cos it gets in through your skin. What's that smell remind you of?'

'Those nuts, almonds.'

'Right. Now, this is gelignite: it's stable—you can drop it, knock and throw it but best not get too cocky. The important thing to remember is that the older it gets the less stable it becomes, but it won't explode without a detonator –that's those tubes over there. As your explosive doesn't become viable until it meets up with its fuse, what can you deduce from that?'

'That we don't bring them together until the last minute?'

'Give me boyo a coconut! Now, those copper fuses are riskier, more sensitive to handle, than the jelly because -pass one over -this tip contains the all-important ultra-sensitive base charge. All we need to bring this little beauty and the bomb to life is a radio signal.'

The long sausage of the explosive, a clay-like gritty orange substance, was tamped, with the handle end of a wooden spoon, into a plastic tube which in turn was inserted into the metal shell of a small empty fire extinguisher. Liam watched as Coyne completed the process.

◆◆◆

Dooley, Liam found, was more approachable than Coyne although he too could be taciturn when the bomb maker was on a rant. Liam decided that Dooley came from better circumstances than Coyne or himself. He was more knowledgeable about things, which perhaps came from all the books he read. He appeared never to be without one.

'Frank, what the feck are we doing here?'

Dooley looked up from making a cigarette. He licked the edge, gave it a short roll and passed it to the seated Liam. He then made a second and lit both with a Swan Vesta.

'Well, I for one, Liam, am watching, and you are the gopher having a day off.'

'No, be serious, why are we down here in the backwoods when all the action is back there across the border?'

'Well, as we sit here on this drystone dike, on the first sunny day for a while, looking across some of Ireland's finest scenery, give it some thought. Logical thought and tell me why you think we are here. First, what have we been doing most of?'

'Well I've watched Coyne making bombs. And I've had weapon train— '

'Stay with bombs. Your training with small arms is basic training for you, which, at this stage, won't be used. Next thought, how often do we come out here and what might we be doing.'

'About every two or three days at different times for the last week. We come here, we chat and after a couple of hours we go back.'

Frank spat a shred of tobacco. Then nodded at the vista before them.

'What do you see between us and the Atlantic?'

'All there is out there is that castle with the tower.'

The older man flicked the nub end of the cigarette into the road and began to roll another.

'Let me tell you about that castle, Liam.'

◆◆◆

Viscount Palmerston, twice Prime Minster of Great Britain, who had an Irish peerage built Classiebawn Castle. No expense was spared on materials, as opposed to the pittance for human labour. The yellow stone of the castle was ferried from Donegal.

It had a chequered history. Not long after the Rising the Republicans held their hostages, taken for exchange of Irish prisoners in Mountjoy Prison, Dublin, within its walls. They made it known they had mined its premises and primed them ready to blow to deter the Government forces from action. When the rebellion ended the Irish Free State housed troops there.

With the creation of the State of Eire, the new government returned it to its owners although rights of ownership of the surrounding ten thousand acres of land was not given back. Throughout the years of its existence the house passed to Palmerston's step son, then from his nephew, who had no direct heir, to the Earl of Salisbury's second son. He passed it to his son who spent his holidays here with his two daughters. One, Edwina, inherited it after his death.

'Any idea who this Edwina was, Liam. No, maybe not. She still comes here with her old man.' Dooley looked at Liam as though expecting an answer and when none was forthcoming, he chuckled.

'Used to be a sailor.'

◆◆◆

One night, after a long day in the garage behind Coyne's barn, they were walking towards the cottage, when they heard the telephone. Coyne broke into a run and entered the cottage leaving the door open for Liam. He waved the younger man through and past him into the living room as he took the call.

Liam had no sooner sunk onto the sofa when the call ended, and Coyne beckoned from the doorway.

'Get the motor. We're on a recce.'

He pulled up in front of the cottage as Coyne emerged, pulling on an anorak. As he climbed in, he dropped a Browning pistol into Liam's lap.

'Don't feckin use this unless I say, understand?' he said.

When Liam did not respond, he snarled,

'Do you feckin understand?'

Liam grunted in the affirmative and nodded. A mollified Coyne sat back in his seat. The Landrover pulled away and they drove in silence for ten minutes before the older man grasped Liam's lower arm and indicated a small lay-by with a nod of his head.

Liam pulled the vehicle over to the side of the road. Coyne sat forward and said, 'He's back.'

At Liam's questioning glance he pointed and said, 'The flag. The flag means he's back in residence. He was here earlier this month but pissed off down to Dublin. Now he's back and ready for the taking.'

Liam looked across the intervening distance, for the umpteenth time since his arrival in the area, at the huge pseudo castle of Classiebawn, made of Mountcharles sandstone, and outlined against the expanse of Donegal Bay behind. There was activity taking place in the building evidenced by the lighted windows all over the front of the edifice. In a flat voice, displaying no curiosity he asked,

'Who is?'

'Admiral of the Fleet, Louis Francis Albert Victor Nicholas George bloody Mountbatten, 1st Earl Mountbatten of Burma, KG, GCB, and enough initials after his name to sink one of his own feckin' battleships.'

Liam held up the pistol and asked,

'And we're to do him now? With this?'

Coyne did not detect the sarcasm in Liam's voice and missed the sideways look the younger man gave him.

'Don't talk daft, you soft gobshite. Look at the forecourt of that place. In front there. Those two cars are An Gardaí Siochana. You're from the North but even you must have heard of these people? Right? Bloody nursemaids. Nah, it would never happen here.'

Liam held his annoyance under control at the patronising tone of his 'mentor', refusing to allow it to show.

'Turn this thing around and head back. We've got work to do.'

Chapter Four

Coyne was restive and it showed. He puffed rapidly on his rolled cigarette, frequently spitting out tobacco shreds. Dooley and Liam did not speak. The telephone broke the silence and he dived across the room to pick it up.

He held it to his ear without a word for five or more minutes then slammed down the receiver.

'Bastards! Indecisive, wavering bastards! Can you bloody believe it? We're set up, ready to go, and now they're having second thoughts!'

Realizing that he was referring to the Staff, Liam kept his mouth shut, but Coyne wanted a more partisan response from those around him. Dooley pushed himself up from the armchair and crossed to the mantelpiece for the tobacco and papers.

'Be fair, Tom, things won't be easy once this takes off. It will galvanise the Brits and have them buzzing about worse than a hornets' nest. There'll be no place to hide.'

'Don't talk feckin' wet, Frank. When's it ever been easy? What more can they do? I've got fifty pounds of bang prepped and wired to go. For the first time, that boat won't be searched or guarded and that cost me a feckin' fortune, I can tell you. Do you realise, if this doesn't take off, I'm out more than a few grand? Do you think they'll refund me then?'

He blew out through clenched teeth. Hand on the mantelpiece, he stared down into the empty grate. Then, mind made up, he turned saying,

'Let's get the damned thing on board, primed and ready to go, and if they change their minds, yet a-feckin-gain, we'll at least have done our bit.'

'So, boyo, this is where you come into your own.' At Liam's questioning look Coyne continued, 'You'll be putting the bomb on the boat.'

'On my own?'

'Yes, on your own. You got a problem with that?'

'No, no way, but I'm only doing it on one condition.'

Coyne couldn't believe his ears. He leaned across the table and grabbed two fistfuls of Liam's shirt front.

'You wee bastard,' he roared, 'I'm your feckin' commander and all you've got to do is obey bloody orders. And my orders--' Coyne broke off as Liam, stronger than he appeared, grasped his wrists and forced him to let go.

'Like I said, one condition. I get to detonate the bomb.'

Dooley placed a restraining hand on Coyne's lower arm to forestall the irate answer

'Tommy, just think. He's done well at his training, seems reliable enough. If he's firing the thing you and me could be miles away if we ever needed an alibi. Think about it.'

After some heavy breathing Coyne nodded to Dooley but turned away from Liam.

'You brief him. The little shite pisses me off.'

◆◆◆

Liam climbed down the steel ladder to the deck of the target, the Shadow V, painted a unique shade of dark green. Once aboard he prised up two planks of the deck between the hatch and the tiller. He replaced the jemmy in his backpack and removed the rolled cloth containing the loaded tube. From a side pocket he extracted the copper detonator and inserted it into the bomb, which he positioned above the propeller shaft below the planks. The planks fitted into their former positions and showed no evidence of disturbance. A glance at his watch told Liam that by leaving now he would be at the cottage as the sun came up.

Coyne and Dooley had left ninety minutes earlier for Granard leaving Liam with the Landrover, to get back into the village and down to the harbour.

Liam took the radio control device from its hiding place in the garage. Opening a pack of batteries, he replaced the existing ones in the remote with the new set. He enjoyed the first of the series of vicarious thrills of power he would experience that day.

Holidaymakers, from north and south of the island, thronged the village streets. Liam could not believe the number of boats out on the water below the wall. He had a moment of doubt when it crossed his mind the sheer number of vessels in the harbour might degrade the strength of his radio signal. He didn't consider the collateral deaths or injuries the projected explosion might cause.

It was too early for the passengers of Shadow V to come to town but not too early to settle the score with Coyne. He crossed the road, entered the phone box and contacted the Gardaí in Granard to report a stolen vehicle.

◆◆◆

The weather could not have been better, with a beautiful clear sky and soft white clouds, all wasted on Liam. From the hillside beyond Mullaghmore his vantage point gave him an uncluttered view of the harbour and its approaches.

He had thought the party from Classiebawn might not be coming when he saw the Gardaí escort car precede the Land Rover onto the quayside. He noticed that there were three young boys and an elderly lady in the group, but he did not care, provided the old man was there--and he was, tall and erect with glowing white hair. Patriarch of the group he was impatient.

The others headed down to the boat. They disappeared to reappear in Liam's vision as Shadow V cleared the side of the dock and made its way seawards.

Liam allowed himself a few seconds of anticipation. This was clout; raw unadulterated power. This wasn't some commonplace nonentity he was snuffing out but someone of importance who had played an integral and famous part in world affairs and, by his passing, would ensure Liam's rise in the hierarchy of the IRA. The thought crossed his mind that getting a target more prominent than this one would be difficult.

He pressed the button. The indicator light turned from green to red and as he raised his head the bomb roared to fill the sky above with planking, chunks of metal and human body parts.

◆◆◆

They came out of the pub to see two members of the Gardaí circling their car.

Coyne, and Dooley with the vehicle keys in his hand, walked towards the vehicle. They ignored the two policemen. Dooley unlocked the driver's door then, leaning on the roof of the car, he addressed the senior of the two standing on the pavement.

'Is there a problem?'

'It would appear so. Don't bother getting in the vehicle, just yet.' He looked at his companion as the man finished speaking in a low voice into his radio. The man nodded and then drew his sidearm.

'Lock the vehicle back up. Then, both of you, face the car and put your hands on the roof.'

◆◆◆

In the station's interview room Coyne frowned at the officer across the desk.

'We're keeping you in custody until we can make further inquiries on the report we've had, that the car was taken without the owner's permission.'

'Stolen! I've got the registration documents to prove it's mine, ye gobshite.'

The officer ignored the seated man's irritation and continued.

'We also have reason to believe you are both active members of a banned organisation. And, in the light of what has just happened up the coast, together with what we have on file about your specific speciality, Mr Coyne, we will carry out further examinations of your persons to see if we find any link to that explosion.'

Coyne blinked and looked down at his hands relieved he washed them after using the bogs in the pub. Then his scalp prickled, and the blood pounded in his temples. He remembered. The fecking latex gloves —the damning rubber gloves —in his jacket pocket.

◆◆◆

Shortly after Mullaghmore, as he broke out of the mire of nonentity, he asked as a reward to be allowed to stay in bomb making. Despite having no previous experience or formalised training, his stay with Coyne and the hours watching the assembly of the devices convinced him of his suitability as an 'engineer'; the name used within the organisation for bomb maker.

Word came down he should report to an ASU in Crossmaglen, South Armagh.

Chapter Five

There was little indication that first day that he would have a meteoric ascent to commanding rank and garner a mythical reputation.

His initial appearance before the Council, as a recognised armourer par excellence, the top 'engineer', was the day of their first clash. He had been ordered to provide a device to destroy or cripple one of the major department stores in Belfast. The Bank Building, part of Belfast's architectural heritage, home to Primark, had had its share of 'mishaps' and survived them all. The current occupiers believed themselves justified in ignoring the IRA's requests for contributions.

The last call for a 'donation' was strongly worded, in effect a demand, and the retaliation, openly stated, should this final request be ignored, would be devastating.

He came in from Armagh to describe his plan to the Council. The reception appeared favourable but not overly enthusiastic. Intuition told Liam that this was down to the Chief of Staff's expression of non-committal. Several desultory questions were asked prior to Diffin clearing his throat and asking Liam to sit down.

The Chief of Staff agreed the physical side of the operation, while not flawless, was adequate. His difficulty with acceptance arose from the political after-effect of such a demonstration due to the increasing, and vocal, opposition to public bombings where the collateral damage was indiscriminate.

Diffin's position, from the nods and demeanour of the others present, was well supported. He proposed a large blast, causing heavy structural damage, but detonated during the night to minimise human deaths or injuries. Liam's strong rebuttal to this counter proposal caused a surprised reaction. Afterwards, he believed that his temerity, as a novice, openly challenging a well-established pillar of the Staff, and not any perceived weakness of his counter argument, prompted the opposing view. The Chief of Staff's subsequent response was devastating, and more so since it was couched in patronising simplified language. That it was delivered in tones of moderation and a total lack of emotive power made it even more forceful. Liam could not control the hot flush that suffused his neck and features, but he bit down and made no answer. The ensuing vote was unanimous.

Liam was tasked to carry out the operation at night. He meekly accepted and stated that he understood his instructions. The job would be carried out as specified.

With one important difference

His plan and preparations to cause an explosion at Primark would not be modified, put on hold or back burnered. He did not appreciate being told to deviate from a scheme in which he had invested time and effort. That his kicking over the traces could backfire, and badly, did not escape him. However, he was confident his recent successes would support his position and his newly found popularity among the rank and file was strong enough for him to survive. He was not a poodle and he had never been susceptible to leashes no matter who was pulling on the other end.

A long delay timer, with a deferment of two days, would work. He had the needed components of the VCR from the Sony he cannibalised. The 'bang' would need twenty to twenty-five pounds to do what he wanted. Gerry, Belfast East's quartermaster, said the Belgian gear Frangex was the only blow he had on the shelf in any quantity. There was twenty-three pounds, but it would do at a push. There would be no problem in its release since orders had already been received from the top to hold it. For him.

He had reconnoitred the clothing department store two days earlier and decided that the best place for the nest would be behind the thin wooden panelling of the display counter near the entrance. The display areas were set up as four-sided hollow squares with a gap in one side to allow the shop assistant access. Each run had alcoves, below the show surface, separated by decorative hollow stretches closed off with painted plywood. It would be a simple job to remove one of the sheets, place the bomb and replace the covering.

The sole security measure during the hours of darkness, was the interior lights that were left on. There was most likely an alarm system, silent or otherwise, linked directly to Musgrave Police Station in Victoria Street. No matter, these things had never been a problem in the past for his crew. He'd get Long to check the place. Provided the system was vulnerable, and he'd finished his assembly by that evening, they'd go for the next night.

He'd set the timer for Saturday.

Why Saturday night, you ask, Mr Diffin? Any night would do, you say? No one is liable to be injured, you think?

True, Mr Diffin, but I didn't say Saturday night. I'm going for Saturday! Midday, to be exact.

◆◆◆

Married for less than a year she had accompanied her husband, a newly qualified G.P. to his first position in a shared practice. It was her first move away from Derry. They had taken on a mortgage of a two bedroomed bungalow on the outskirts of Belfast, fast becoming her favourite city. Shopping was one of the highlights of her week and the best part was looking. It wasn't necessary to buy anything to enjoy it but, she smiled, her husband wouldn't agree.

The rain had stopped so she closed her telescopic brolly and dropped it in her wicker shopping basket. She moved out of the way as more shoppers from the next bus surged onto the pavement. As the vehicle pulled away, she could see the clock on the tower.

'Twelve o'clock, just the right time to …

The thought was never completed. She had her back to the shop when the bomb exploded. Shoes, pullovers, ornamental window dressings and plastic limbs of the dissected tailor's dummies, in a cruel, immediate parody of the butchered human bodies hurtled into the street.

Mrs Helen Devlin née Rath, Declan's younger sister, did not feel the tremendous blow in the small of her back. She lost consciousness. Death and darkness came from a huge shard of granite masonry that pulverised her spine and crushed her rib cage.

◆◆◆

When called to account at the subsequent inquiry Liam blatantly lied and explained the explosion as premature due possibly to a defective grade of wire or time degraded explosive. He apologised for any mistake and took full responsibility. It was accepted but it was to the first of several instances where his throwing over the traces brought him in conflict with the leadership.

Chapter Six

Liam believed he had his Eureka moment with the scheme for proxy bombings. The spate of premature detonations, suffered by the IRA's bombers, with the resultant indiscriminate loss of life, frequently including the death of a Volunteer 'courier', was rising. Although the organisation could ill afford to lose members without a corresponding toll of the enemy's forces there was also a collateral degradation of the IRA's image. Even among its own supporters in the Republican community snide jokes were rife every time an explosion occurred prior to reaching its scheduled target. The British Army had coined the term 'own goal' for these accidents and it caused extreme embarrassment when it was used in national headlines.

It was no recent phenomenon. The inherent danger in having non-specialists handle explosive devices with ensuing mishaps was a long running sore. As far back as the late fifties when the loss of four men, and their weapons, not to mention the death of a civilian and destruction of his cottage, in Edentubber, was a disaster. Lackadaisical prepping, a faulty alarm clock and naivety with land mines contributed to the fiasco. Despite warnings in what not to do their death was portrayed as self-sacrifice and martyrdom. Liam recognised it for what it was –

an unnecessary fuck-up. A bomb of that magnitude on the streets could have created havoc. However, like Patton maintained, there was no percentage in dying for your country; the whole point was to make the enemy die for his. As one of the staunchest supporters of the bombing campaigns, due in no small way, to his own bomb making expertise, he was aggrieved at the perceived slur on bomb makers and by association his reputation.

The loss of life among the carriers could be minimised if there were a new 'delivery system'.

He had come up with what he believed to be the ultimate answer.

Joseph Grogan had done time in his youth. Frequent truancy compounded his learning difficulties. Petty thieving, small scale burglaries and the occasional mugging, together with the unenviable misfortune of being apprehended and charged each time, had resulted in a criminal record. This made it difficult to get a decent job. Being born a Catholic added to the predicament.

Taken on by the British Army, albeit as an unskilled labourer, two years earlier, had been a Godsend. Married, with small children, he was a surprisingly loving and caring father and did his best, with lapses, to be a dutiful husband. His wife Mary worked as a cleaning woman at the Army base, having been given consideration for employment because he already worked there. With the combined wages they were able to survive — just. Now, their regular income was threatened by what MacDermot was demanding. It was unreasonable. He couldn't agree to it.

'Christ, I've got three wee uns. I can't just walk away from my job. There's nothing else coming in.'

'Get on benefits the same as the others!'

'Can't afford to. There's no money for at least six weeks if I voluntarily chuck it. I've only got two years on the job and was looking for the bonus coming up. Christmas is nearly here. Will you make up the difference? Pay a wage until I get the dole money?'

The questions were ignored.

'You're a Catholic but to keep working on the base for the British makes you a collaborator in our eyes. If you'll not pack it in, we can't be responsible for what happens next.'

'Jasus! I'm in the cookhouse. A skivvy. I'm just a labourer.'

'I've made it as clear as I can you're considered a traitor and as such liable to be dealt with as one. That's it, final. Stop or take the consequences. Now, on your way.'

'But please I need...'

'Conversation over. On your bike.'

'For the love of— '

'Git te fuck! Or do you want kneecapping!'

◆ ◆ ◆

'Mary, they'll no do it. They can't go around kneecapping or topping everybody. There's twelve of us Catholics on that base.'

Mrs Grogan wiped her tears with her pinny. The youngest started to cry, intimidated by stress and fear he could hear in his parent's voices. She bent to pick him up.

'But you can't be sure, Billy, you can't.'

'What's the alternative? Tell me that, love; I just wish you could – I'm at my wit's end.'

Later that evening, the front door, leading directly into their small front room from outside, slammed back against the wall. Mrs Grogan screamed in terror as four masked and armed men barrelled into the sitting room. The leader struck her husband across the bridge of the nose with the butt of his automatic and two of the others grabbed an arm each and dragged him through the open door to the street and into the waiting van.

◆◆◆

Through badly bruised lips he tried to respond but no sound came out.

'I feckin' asked you if you understood, you gobshite. Feckin' answer! Do you understand? You drive the van, with the bang to the checkpoint. You stop at the barrier. Turn off the engine, make sure you take out the key, then jump out and leg it. You'll have three minutes before the lot detonates.' With each sentence the heel of the butt came down forcibly on Grogan's knee.

'And why will you do this? Because if you don't, we're going nut you. The others that were left with your wife and kids will do likewise with them. Now, once again, do you understand what you have to do?'

Grogan licked his upper lip, tasting the salt of the sweat mingled with the metallic taste of the dried blood. He tried to swallow but couldn't. He gagged and wanted to plead but daren't.

'I'm losing patience wi you! Answer before I just up and top you here and now!'

'I – I unnerstan, I do. Don't hit me agin. I 'll do what I have to do.'

There were two armed sentries, wearing flak jackets and helmets immediately in front of the gate with four more, two on either side of the road, watching his approach. He looked in the side mirror and saw that the car was some distance away with his captors, and the remote trigger, ready to detonate one thousand pounds of homemade explosive stacked behind him. He took his hand from the steering wheel and wiped the sweat from his forehead. Some trickled over his eyebrows and stung his eyes. He re-gripped the wheel and took a huge breath.

The barrier was raised and the car in front, cleared for entry to the base, moved forward. One of the sentries lifted an arm and beckoned him onwards. He put the vehicle back into gear, released the handbrake and let the clutch engage.

In the escorting vehicle, the driver turned to Liam in the passenger seat taking in the fact that his hands were empty.

'Are you getting the remote ready? For after he jumps out?'

'There's no need.'

Liam leaned forward as the driver's side door of the van opened. Grogan's right leg reached outwards. In the infinitesimal pause before his foot could reach the ground the cabin's interior light system carried the charge to the detonator. The metal of the van and barrier, the concrete of the nearby guardhouse, the rags of the uniforms and the flesh of the victims blossomed into the air to be scattered over several acres of Ayrshire Barracks.

◆◆◆

'Without clearance or permission — '

'Since when did I need permission to kill Brits?' Liam snarled down at the seated Diffin. Each of the men on either side of the Chief of Staff stared impassively at the standing Commander.

'Your efforts have single-handedly scuppered much of the support that we depend upon in this struggle. The sheer cold blooded — '

'Oh, fer Christ sake! The movement condones violence and that's the only way those feckers are going to be driven from the island. I'll— '

'Shut the fuck up, MacDermot,' roared Diffin springing to his feet and leaning across the table to thrust his face next to Liam's 'just shut the fuck up and listen.' He expelled breath heavily, then lowering himself back in his chair, coughed then continued.

'For a start you've always had carte blanche in selecting targets and engaging the enemy, which you've done up to now with no one complaining at the results. However, you ignored the recent directive that all operations have to be sanctioned by the Staff. This latest episode has drastic consequences for us all. Bishop Daly and many, many others in the Church are horrified and shocked —.' He raised an admonishing finger as Liam attempted to interrupt.

'Our support in the States has taken a shellacking with a massive drop off in donations and the Boston Times report, describing the bombing as unmitigated savagery, triggered thousands of protesting letters from its readers. Much of the sympathy we had from our own over there has evaporated. The mistake in all this, bringing this shit storm down on us, was your mindless, brain dead action in coercing a Catholic man with three kiddies to make the final sacrifice while we sit on the side-lines.'

'We sit on the side-lines?' shouted MacDermot, 'I was feckin' there! I'm never on the feckin' side-lines. I'm always in the thick of it. And you lot?'

The men, flanking Diffin across the table, for the first time, responded with startled expressions, the impassive masks vanishing at the South Armagh commander's loud retort. Diffin stood and closed the folder in front of him.

'This is getting nowhere, Liam, you obviously believe you can do no wrong. Since you refuse to listen and present no justification for this catastrophe this hearing is closed. I can assure you this is not finished, far from it. How successful we are in damage limitation will dictate the next steps. You can go!'

◆◆◆

As the days elapsed and weeks passed Liam heard no more complaints from the Staff but suspected it had not been forgotten. He received the request to prepare a proposal for a new initiative for an operation to be in place and ready to implement when the current truce ruptured. He submitted his plan and within two days received the summons.

◆◆◆

The street was empty except for two youngsters kicking a grubby grey tennis ball back and forth. They had seen him. And they had passed a signal, to the watcher in the window. He had not seen it, but he knew the protocols. A stranger to this part of the Bogside, he had never been to any of the terraced houses. The houses had no visible numbers. However, it had to be the one that had wing mirrors fitted to the upstairs window frame that gave the occupants sight of visitors without revealing the fact.

The door was painted an oily green with intermingled brown streaks reminiscent of a wino's vomit. Facing it he waited. There was no need to knock. He heard the thump of feet descending the stairs and a moment later Craven appeared. With the door held half-open Diffin's minder leaned out, looking up and down the street before stepping back to allow Liam to squeeze past. The visitor had already started to mount the stairs when Craven said, 'They're upstairs.'

On the landing Liam turned to Craven, as the other reached the last step, and looked at him in in question. A silent nod towards the first door answered his unspoken query. Craven was not known for good humour and as Liam's relationship with Diffin, his boss, was not one of mutual admiration or respect, he did not need to be other than coldly civil to the man from Armagh.

As he grasped the handle and pushed the door open the waft of acrid fumes from O'Riordan's Gauloise stung his nasal passages.

'So, it's going to be that kind of meet. Just needs Cosoleto.' The inquisitor's body odour was a standing joke among the rank and file.

The room was cramped with little space for the three men seated round the table. An empty chair, its back to the door and opposite Diffin at the table's head, was obviously intended for him. Without turning or taking his eyes off the Chief of Staff Liam tried to close the door behind him. His attempt was blocked by Craven who had squeezed into the limited space behind him.

No one spoke. O'Riordan and Cosoleto, one at either side of the table, both studied their clasped hands while Diffin continued to stare at Liam, who spoke first.

'So, —?'

'At least sit, Liam. How are you?'

He tilted the wooden chair sideways and pivoted it on one of its rear legs and sat down, adjusting its distance from the table. Positioning himself so that his back was to the left-hand corner of the room he beckoned Craven to come forward into his sight line. Only after the man had squeezed past and located himself at Diffin's shoulder did Liam return his attention to the speaker. Cosoleto and O'Riordan watched with apparent indifference.

'So?'

'As tart as ever. Pleasantries considered a waste of time?'

'True, and especially two-faced trivialities. You've always been the politician and able to oil the proceedings with smarm. I'm not.'

At the open hostility in the response Diffin shrugged, cleared his throat and leaned forward.

'Alright, Liam, let's see if I can put this plainly. It's not going to happen. Your plan has been considered and found lacking. It is not what we want. Nowhere near. You were tasked to plan a new initiative. You had the parameters laid out for you. You told us you understood that we wanted a program not necessarily radically changed but different. Then you come up with a shite proposal. I can't help thinking that you are locked into that mad dog syndrome of bomb them back into the Stone Age. Can't you recognise the self-defeating element of that? If all the targets were military, it might be considered worthwhile. But it is Irish men and women who are suffering.

At the start of the campaign, bombing was a necessity. Your plan to take it to the mainland was nothing short of brilliant but we're in a new phase. The bombing had its place and initially provided the impetus and attention our cause needed, but for some time now no longer has a value. It has served its purpose.'

Liam's eyes never left Diffin's. In his response he bit his words off.

'They're on the back foot. They realise they can't finish us and every day we are proving unbeatable. Irish lives *are* what this is about. It's to make them better that we're doing this; to get the independence everyone says they want. To get the British the fuck out! So, yes, there's a price to pay - even if it is Irish blood. But, if you're so worried, I can take this back to the mainland,' Liam conceded.

'And get the Manchester backlash all over again? Liam, we are just as determined as you are to see this through but perception's growing, in our own ranks even, that the indiscriminate mayhem your bombs are causing non-combatants, including those kids in Manchester, is not worth the candle. It's been —'

'So, they are my bombs now. I'm the only armourer?'

'Liam, you're not obtuse, but you can give a good impression of being so!' Diffin's increasing annoyance was evident in his tone and delivery. 'You are the problem, Liam. The others follow orders and accept the policies we lay down. You are becoming a hindrance. You've never been one to co-operate, let alone concede and your obstinacy is wearing thin for the Staff.'

Liam chuckled mirthlessly. 'The Staff! You mean the other wallies like these two dummies?' To give them their due they didn't react to his disdain but continued to look at him without expression.

Liam shifted his gaze and looked past Diffin across the rooftops towards Creggan. He had no intention of following the orders of this prat with his affectations, and his pompous pontifications about peace instead of a red-blooded thirst for victory.

'You've been straightforward in your opinions for once,' he said slowly. 'And will I, as the problem, be solved in the way it is normally done?'

Cosoleto shifted in his seat as though he had become conscious that he might be called upon to act. As the current head of the 'Nutting Squad', their own version of the Inquisition, he was not known for his intellect. His working experience in Belmont's abattoir had long since deadened any squeamish tendencies he may have had.

Diffin frowned then clasped his hands in front of him.

'We're adults, Liam, there's been no suggestion that it will ever come to that but be warned the agreed way forward will be the Staff's way. There can be no equivocation.'

'John,' said Liam, using the anglicised version of other man's given name in insult, 'I've never trusted you. Your using words like that is only one of the many reasons. You're not really one of us. You've never had any bottle. It is clear you and the others like you are going to flush each sacrifice, every achievement, down the drain. Throw it all away. I ask myself why? To warm your arse in a cushy position in Stormont when it all goes back to the way it always was?

Do what you have to do and bollocks to you.'

The chair tipped towards the door as he stood up. Rather than throw it against the wall, or in anger at Diffin, he caught it deftly with one hand and replaced it. Without another word he left and took to the stairs.

◆◆◆

Due to the convoluted nature of the roads he concentrated on his driving until he was heading toward Glenshane and the A6. Regurgitation of what had happened at the meeting pushed all else from his mind. Unconsciously, he gritted his teeth and increased pressure on the accelerator as his anger, which he had held in check until then, brimmed over. The A6 had morphed into the M22 when the sight of the patrol car on the hard shoulder brought him back and he rapidly reduced speed.

◆◆◆

In his flat overlooking the decorative lampposts on the Albert Bridge he opened the medicine cabinet and swallowed several painkillers followed by gulps of water from his palm. His headache was worse than any migraine he had suffered and was only marginally lessened when he turned out the lights and made his way in the dark to bed.

The turmoil in his mind would not settle but its ebb and flow kept beat with the dull throb of the headache. Slowly, however, sleep did come, and like lava, inched inexorable over his consciousness and brought the inevitable red glow of smothering dreams.

◆◆◆

He had been the South Armagh's Brigade commander for two years and had major successes against the British; one of his ASU's brought down and destroyed one of their helicopters, a first in the war. On his watch they had used a Barrack Buster against an RUC police station to great effect. But his sense of accomplishment was marred, by the competitive challenge presented by the East Tyrone Brigade's actions which were as numerous and as effective as any of those of his organisation. It was commanded by his former mentor and role model

Ciarán McCormack. He advocated a strategy of destroying bases and preventing them being rebuilt or repaired to 'deny ground' to the British occupiers. Several construction bosses had paid with their lives for taking the British coin. Ciarán's Brigade was active mainly in eastern County Tyrone and neighbouring parts of County Armagh and was one of the IRA's most aggressive formations.

The attack on the RUC station at The Birches in 1986 where they had had shot up the police station with machine-gun fire and then severely damaged it with homemade bombs was one of those successes. The perimeter fence had been breached with a digger with a bomb in its bucket.

He met Ciarán on a liaison visit which was to have extensive ramifications for both. He had gone ostensibly to brief his colleague on a proposed hands-off but effective trigger for bombs that he had devised for use in future actions. Instead he'd been co-opted to help in a planned assault on Loughgall RUC station. They needed backup and support and Liam agreed to supply additional men provided he could participate. He accepted that it was to be East Tyrone's party.

They had met in Ciarán's bar in Moortown, County Tyrone. He was behind the bar and came around to greet him at the door and took him through to the snug which was empty.

'What'll you have, Liam' he asked after they had shaken hands.

'I'll have a Schweppes'

'Still not drinking? Christ, I'm hope this doesn't catch on, could make a pauper out of me.' They both laughed.

Drinks in hand they sat at the table next to the fireplace. After some desultory small talk Ciarán described his plan for the strike on Loughgall's police station. It was straight forward and identical to the successful offensive against The Birches.

'We already have a digger spotted, backhoe loader. That'll take us through the perimeter fence with the 350 lb. of Semtex inside an oil drum, covered up with rubble and wired to a couple of 40-second fuses.'

'How many run that place, Ci?'

'Well, it's run part time by three RUC, normally. We've got the opening times. The object is to take them out when they close for the day then wreck the shop. Anyway,' he continued, irritated to be interrupted mid-flow by the question. 'There'll be eight of us in the frame and I'll need your boys for watch and scout duties.'

'And what do you have in mind for me?'

'We won't be wearing our own stuff but will want to be out of that other shit immediately afterwards, so we'll need our normal clothes at hand.'

'So, I'm in charge of wardrobe,' asked Liam put out by the triviality of the nature of his assigned task. Ciarán gave a brief nod and didn't enlarge on his answer.

'Another Schweppes? No? OK. We'll hit it with two teams, one with the digger and one in the van, which'll do the shoot-up. That's the van we lifted from Dungannon.'

'Where's the bomb being put together?'

'The boys at Ardboe. It'll come across the lough, to miss the roadblocks, and we'll bring it from Magherry. We'll come into Loughgall, bomb and van, from the Portadown end through the village then pour it into them.' Ciarán sat back, picking up his Guinness and asked, 'What do you think?'

Liam thought for a moment not answering straight away.

'Three hundred plus of bang for three local plods. Bit on the heavy side, isn't it?' The bar owner frowned, chewed his lip then retorted

'Well, that's the plan.'

'And the ignition?'

'The bomb? Hand job. Zippo to the fuse.'

Liam didn't comment.

◆◆◆

In Holyrood Barracks, in the dining hall, which had been cleared and secured, a briefing for an impending operation was taking place. The commander had the floor and was addressing the SAS soldiers in the conference room.

'The intel is that Paddy's gearing up to do the three-man police shop in Loughgall. Which is here.' The briefing officer's finger indicated the location on the wall map.

'Since they had a successful outing at the Birches, they are doing a repeat with their JCB torpedo act and are going to use a digger to deliver one of their primed milk churns or oil drums in the vehicle's bucket. They'll crash the perimeter fence, shoot up the three plods and bomb the shit out of the station. Then it's off to the local shebeen to celebrate. Except, we'll be there, waiting. Sergeant Grieves will tell you the specific roles you'll play but we'll have some of you in the station in civilian drag and the bulk of you will be in full battle order staked out under the cover of darkness the night before. It'll be a long set as they have it timed for about 7pm.

We're told some of them will be wearing flak jackets which are unlikely to stop any of ammo we're using but nevertheless go for headshots wherever possible.

A bit of additional info. 14 Company's C.O. had a fax from the P.M. Maggie gets updated on all scheduled ops and the fax was related to a briefing she had about this one. It consisted of just two letters. NP. That is obviously open to interpretation, but we've decided to read it as 'No Prisoners'. Need I say more?'

Spider was not one of the six in plain clothes who were to be inside the station with the policemen but was selected to make up the group of the uniformed eighteen lying up in five positions throughout the wooded areas around the building. They set up the three-point triangular formation designed to eliminate everybody in the 'kill zone' while reducing the risk of friendly fire.

◆◆◆

Ciarán and his seven East Tyrone men, arrived in Loughgall from the north-east in a two-vehicle convoy and made two slow passes of the building at seven in the evening.

All were armed, wearing balaclavas, boiler suits, surgical gloves and socks over their footwear to limit evidence of their presence at the scene. The digger drove past the police station, turned around and drove back again. The Toyota van carrying the main IRA assault party did the same, in anticipation of the lightly manned station's staff coming out of the building to go home, thereby presenting themselves as targets. Two gunmen exited the van and joined the driver on the digger, with weapons in one hand and a lighter in the other.

Some minutes after seven they launched the action driving the digger towards the station. The remaining five members of the unit followed in the van with Ciarán in the passenger seat. The excavator ploughed through the light perimeter fence and the fuses were lit. The van stopped a short distance ahead and three of the team jumped out and opened fire at the police station with automatic weapons. At the same time, the bomb detonated, with the blast destroying the digger and badly damaging the building.

◆ ◆ ◆

Immediately, the waiting SAS, inside the building and hidden around the outside area laid down sheets of fire and turned the area around the van and damaged digger into a killing zone. The eight members of the raiding party were slaughtered in a hail of high velocity rounds from Heckler and Koch G3 rifles and two L7A2 GP machine guns. In the abattoir of Loughgall Police Station forecourt the living were reduced to butchered carcasses. All had multiple body lacerations, and all had head wounds. They were literally cut to pieces.

Two brothers, with no connection to the IRA, were collateral damage as they unwittingly drove their white Citroen into the melee; one was killed the other seriously wounded. The dead man chanced to be wearing a boiler suit like those of the downed IRA attackers.

◆◆◆

Liam, in a state of unusual amazement, stared at the brief but horrific scene of mayhem from his car. Tasked to extricate the attackers and pass out the clothing on completion of the operation he was now a superfluous bystander. The riddled corpses, blood soaked dead puppets in rag bundles, littered the station yard. Despite his skill and propensity at delivering Armageddon with his explosive creations he had never been present to see the aftermath of any of them. He was mesmerized and awed. With an effort he yanked his thoughts into a semblance of order. There was nothing he could do here. He engaged gear and turned the wheel to drive off when he found himself staring down the barrel of a rifle in the hands of a masked SAS soldier.

◆◆◆

Spider advanced with the others towards the yard but broke away when he saw the Ford driven by a solitary occupant pull up. His first thought was that the man was a 'peripheral'; a member of the group but operating in a support role. The man's face was devoid of expression, causing the suspicion Spider felt to strongly increase.

◆◆◆

Liam felt a motion in his bowels and had an urgent need to urinate. He bit his lip to prompt control.

'This bastard's going to kill me.'

In all his years of creating and delivering destruction he had never experienced direct confrontation where the threat jeopardised him. He had never seen the whites of their eyes. This was a first and the panic locked his limbs. He pushed down the involuntary retch that threatened to erupt. He held the SAS man's stare but blinked when he heard and realised the implication of the isolated shots from the courtyard.

◆◆◆

Spider considered quickly. He was about to do a double tap and put two rounds automatic through the windscreen when a car containing an elderly couple pulled up behind the car in front of him. Overhead the approaching helicopter started its descent bringing the regular soldiers in who would secure and maintain the site. It was time to pull out. He heard the call to assemble for evacuation. He gesticulated to the drivers of both cars to turn around and drive off. Flicking the safety catch on his weapon he turned away to join the others.

◆◆◆

Liam's whole being slumped, and the rigidity oozed from of his body. He sagged like a rag doll. He knew the SAS git had known he was involved. How had he avoided being 'emptied'? With a partly nervous, and totally relieved laugh, he regained control. As a lapsed Catholic he had no faith in an all seeing and protective deity, but his agnosticism had been brought to the brink that evening.

◆◆◆

Diffin stopped writing and gazed reflectively at the icon of Jesus on the wall. His thoughts were far from religion, however, and focused on the thorn in *his* side. MacDermot. *Man from Armagh my arse*!

He had never liked MacDermot but admitted his aversion stemmed from his initial impressions of the man. MacDermot, at their first meeting, was arrogant and dismissive. He had been loath to listen to the views of others. Content only to propound his theory of wide scale bombing as the road to victory and to the detriment of any other options. He did not hide his scorn for those Volunteers who were not members of active cells.

And yet it was difficult to minimise his contributions to the cause. He was, no, is, a Jack of all trades but competent to the nth degree in all fields. A bombmaker par excellence, his inventiveness together with the effectiveness of his creations, had contributed in no small way to the success of the IRA as a worthy opponent of the British. MacDermot's opposition, as South Armagh senior commander, to the cell structure, which he instituted throughout the Organisation, provided another reason of why they clashed. The cell structure was undoubtedly the most secure system, compartmentalising the whole into watertight units, and would prevent haemorrhaging of intel.

He sighed.

Except it didn't.

The issue of the directive, his directive, that all operations had to be centrally approved had negated the utility of close security. It meant more individuals had sight of suggested actions as the proposals were forwarded up the chain.

Under MacDermot's leadership the South Armagh battalions outshone all the other units. They had one or two notable failures, but their successes were memorable. They were cohesive and, in most cases, deadly. They provided much of the ingenuity and application in the forays his organisation had made into the heartlands of the British. Canary Wharf and Manchester had been of mixed PR value. As events they appeared brutal and savage, but they had enormous effect on the enemy's morale and self-belief. It was brought home to them that they could be hurt. Importantly, public opinion was levered in support of withdrawal from the North. In effect MacDermot and his support from Armagh was key to many of the successes.

But it all came back to his one major failing – he was not a team player. His disobedience and failure to accept the majority rule was disruptive. Something would have to been done and soon. He would cut the Gordian knot.

◆◆◆

Liam sat in his car outside the pub. He was early for his appearance before the Council, who would assemble in the functions room, where the disciplinary review board would present its findings. His future had been determined and the result would be known by everyone in a short while.

He thought about the debacle in Loughgall and the inevitable conclusion that his idol had feet of clay. The infallibility in which he had cloaked his hero had evaporated like steam from a kettle. The shambles was inexcusable but then, he admitted to himself, for the first time, Ciarán had never been open to the suggestions of others. And yet, he couldn't attribute all the blame for the failure to East Tyrone's dead commander. The lack of training, scarcity of planning and bad intel throughout the organisation had become glaringly apparent. His conclusion was that the deficiency was a deliberate ploy by the leadership to negate the strength of the armed struggle in favour of a political solution -and jobs for the boys in the structure to be established by Sinn Fein – *and the never to be got rid of perfidious Brits. God! I hate those shits —and Diffin!*

◆◆◆

The members of the Council were stony-faced as Sean Diffin, Chief of Staff, announced the outcome. Had he imagined it or was that a smirk that flitted across O'Riordan's face? He, Liam MacDermot, had been removed from the Staff. *One fucking vote! One bloody casting vote. Diffin again!* The possibility of the exclusion had always existed, but not its probability. Now it was here, crashing down on him like an avenging thunderbolt. To his chagrin, it was patently obvious he had woefully underestimated Diffin's capacity and power base. He had been overconfident in his own ability to drum up support within the organisation.

He had refused to follow the policy of 'easing off'. His reluctance, his refusal, might have been tolerated had he not again actively demonstrated his disagreement. A bomb he had made, a roadside land mine that he had also put in place, had destroyed a van carrying fourteen workers who had been re-building a British Army base in Omagh. To Liam, it was a legitimate target. Eight dead and four seriously injured. All Protestant collaborators. But to no avail. Diffin said he would 'have to be brought to heel'. This particularly rankled as the man had no active service in his meteoric rise to his present position. He was a political animal, pure and simple, with his strong ties to the kingmakers in Sinn Fein. Diffin had never taken to Liam-had never been impressed- as others were, with the feats of derring-do, some almost suicidal, that he had accomplished while in the field.

It was nauseating. He had been an excellent soldier, and leader, over the years and. He had never lost sight of his own ambitions but had still contributed immeasurably to achieving the aims of the organisation. The months spent in Libya, in the godforsaken desert, learning the advances of the modern bomb maker's craft only for these nonentities to discount his sacrifices. He'd overseen training, often for days at a time, in the damp, sodden countryside of Armagh, with bunches of country bumpkins, that he had changed into all-round militia, capable of mounting effective ambushes. Dedicated, comprehensive realistic training to set up actions that made the world press by their sheer audacity. As Commander of the South Armagh Brigade he had put himself at risk as a sniper and trained and developed the skills of the embryo sharpshooters under his command making them the most feared element in Armagh for Brit foot patrols.

As an interrogator he had uncovered informants and Judases. To have his reputation and rank destroyed by these sheep-heads, for being a soldier and not a compromise seeking coward? Drummed out for not being a feckin' wimp? Christ, he was 'The Man from Armagh'!

The wrath tightened his rib cage and intense heat suffused his neck and face. He returned to staring at the table. Now that he had seen Diffin's look of distaste, he refused to look at the faces of the others.

'Liam, it goes without saying that this decision has not been easy for any of us. However, now that it has been made, you should accept it is effective immediately. Your intractable opposition to our agreed policy makes it impossible for you to remain a member of this Staff. You will retain your position as Commandant of South Armagh but will no longer have a vote or place at this table. Your successor will be in touch, within the next two days, to finalise the arrangements.' *Successor! So, whoever he was, he was already standing in the wings waiting for the corpse to be trolleyed out! Liam* maintained his composure and kept his face motionless, devoid of expression.

Replaced, fecking deposed and trashed, by you worthless gobshites! Who do you think you are? Arseholes! And all because of a policy of compromise and rapprochement with the scrofulous, shit-eating British! And that because Diffin used his special vote to break the deadlock! Again!

He was asked to stand, which he did, and stood behind his chair with his hands resting, lightly, on the back of it. *Control is everything, give no fecking indication!*

'Commandant MacDermot, the movement will be eternally grateful to you for your contributions. It is unfortunate that new times require new approaches. Tiochfaidh ár lá.'

'Beidh do lá teacht.' *Oh yes, your fucking day will come. You can bank on that.*

Peace process! The sheer futility of it all enraged him. Years, lifetimes of fighting against the British wasted! Why would anybody, least of all, the relatives of those who had already died, want this kind of peace? It would be as if the whole rising had never happened. More relevant, it made all that had passed, pointless.

He thought back to his mentor and guru Ciarán McCormack, and what the likelihood of appeasement would be if he were in charge instead of the gutless Diffin. As he now realised McCormack had not been the most astute of men but was possessed of a lion's heart and certainly no quitter.

What had been gained? *A halt to the carnage, they bleated.* But what had been achieved? What had been the point of the war? There was no answer, and that was the sickening aspect. But it wouldn't remain that way if he had anything to do with it.

It was time for him to put into effect a plan that had been fermenting in his mind for longer than he cared to admit. On occasion he had experienced real disappointment that the time had not been right for his project. Now he was glad, ecstatic even, that the wipe-out, the destruction of this peace process endeavour, would result from the action he planned.

The Mullaghmore affair in those early days had had nothing to do with him in a strategic capacity but did motivate him. The follow-up furore in the media and the publicity it brought to the struggle still excited him. One of its failings might have been when the Brit turds came to the table shaken in resolve, the opportunity to press the advantage home was missed by his ball-fumbling colleagues. This failure played a large part in the current nauseating peace process where compromise was the best they could hope for. A similar, or better and more spectacular event, might very well reverse the process so that only total victory by one side or the other would be acceptable.

Chapter Seven

Within a day of their return to the base in Metkovic, Spider and Declan realised their continued presence in Croatia was untenable. Rumours of what happened became widespread. Little or none of it factual; the truth underwent so much flamboyant embroidery it developed beyond all recognition and credibility. This would not have been a problem if the authorities had treated the stories as fanciful gossip. They had not.

Smuggling, within UNHCR, on a cottage industry scale, existed for as long as the organisation itself. One aspect of UNHCR's ethos, its altruism, was a myth. The uninhibited delivery of charitable aid delivered across many varied borders to the needy occurred, but in performance fostered the illegal trafficking. Many group members, of all nationalities, supplemented their not insubstantial incomes with the prohibited ferrying of contraband. The unlawful passage of in-demand goods was endemic. Commodities, such as coffee, washing powder, cigarettes, much desired by black marketeers in the war-torn areas, formed the major part of the contraband. Convoy drivers were ideal for this mode of trafficking. UNHCR tolerated the action, if not ignoring it.

Allegations, however, appeared in press reports, describing the flow of weapons, in both directions, across fluid borders. Pistols, Kalashnikovs, the occasional grenade came into the hands of malcontents outside the Balkans and quantities, on a massive scale, reached the combatants on all sides in the war zones. For obvious reasons, among them the smear on UNHCR humanitarian ideals, such activity was unacceptable. Any doubt cast on the integrity of the Commissioner's office impacted on the financial support received and on revenue funding the charities supporting the organisation. UNHCR's management, however, identified with life's realities. Since it could not eradicate the trafficking the first line of defence was to discredit, then bury, if possible, any such reports. Total eradication continued to be unachievable. To minimize, or even impede the bootlegging, would require resources not available; easier to deny its existence.

A displeased Head of Station (HOS) questioned Spider. Harsh criticism from Geneva, relating to the deaths of two of his, and hence *her*, drivers made the HOS more than a little reluctant to refer the smuggling of weapons and ammunitions up the chain. Spider persuaded her that none of the personnel in her aegis of operations took any part in the planned shipping of the weapons, knew nothing of the smuggled freight, and had not profited by delivery of that cargo. She conceded he and the others on the convoy may have been duped; but only when he emphasised that so too had she.

It came as no surprise, however, that to avoid detrimental speculation, UNHCR no longer required the services of the company. Substantial termination payments to all involved sweetened the bitterness this pill caused. The parent organisation and owner of the vehicles and equipment reacted with alacrity to UNHCR's bleat of outrage. Three representatives arrived to close the outfit and salvage what remained of the company's reputation. The lucrative contracts placed by UNHCR merited the effort. To get their share of future business they would have to minimize the damage caused to their reputation and regain an unblemished image.

Both men had built up a tight circle of good friends among the 'on-the-road' element of UNHCR's community. Many of the other companies would willingly take them as employees as it was well known they were reliable and dedicated to getting convoys through. However, neither Rath nor Spider considered remaining in the Balkans. They may have found positions with any of the other outfits supplying humanitarian aid but obtaining the essential passes and clearances for each of them, from UNHCR, would without doubt, be difficult if not downright impossible.

It was best to move on.

◆◆◆

They packed their gear, loaded it in Spider's Audi, and travelled up-country to Zagreb. Rath planned to go to Germany, travel within the country and see some of the places he had read about. After some time in Berlin, to see the remains of the Wall, he wanted to tour the former East Germany. Leipzig and Dresden together with Weimar were high on his list. After going north to Hamburg, he would detour to Munich, enjoy the sights there before going to see Siobhan, the attractive leader of the IRA cell in Frankfurt.

Spider convinced that he would not visit this part of Croatia again, intended to enjoy travelling the scenic route along the western coast one last time; to catch the ferry crossing the Adriatic then, motoring northwards, the Channel port. He would be glad to see Blighty again, but without desperation or any desire to hurry.

A strong bond, despite their initial enmity, had developed between the two men during their time in Croatia and Bosnia. They agreed to meet in London after settlement of their immediate personal affairs. Co-operating again, since they worked well in tandem, was on the cards. Whilst making no final decision both agreed they were active and fit enough, so they could pursue a future together that might involve risk. There would always be a market for protection, such as body guards, protective escorts, security, and, dependent on clients, a lucrative one. London, a major metropolis for the rich and famous, seemed an obvious choice as a base. Spider possessed several friends and acquaintances from his service days who had translated and adapted their military training and expertise into a much-desired service by the élite of the capital.

◆◆◆

After dropping Rath at the central station in the capital to catch his train to Germany, Spider drove the battered Audi out of the city towards Karlovac, then onward to Senj and the coastal highway. He experienced a pang of unexpected nostalgia driving along the road they had used, when based near Zagreb, to reach Metkovic and the crossing into Bosnia.

The round trip added two days to their itinerary in convoy. For expediency the whole convoy group moved, lock, stock and barrel to the southern town of Metkovic, halving their time on the road by making faster deliveries and reduced turn round time.

A drive of several hours lay ahead of him after which he would take the midnight ferry from Dubrovnik. The vessel docked in the port of Bari, Italy early next morning where, refreshed after the rest, he'd leave the ship. Then, it would be up the leg of Italy, through the Bremer Pass to the Channel terminal and home.

The sight of the coastal town of Senj in the early sunshine as he crested the slope moved him more than he would care to admit. He pulled over to take in the raw beauty of the red roofs and wide expanse of blue sea. It brought back the memory of his first stint as convoy leader, when the drivers parked in the harbour area for a rest interval. One driver, a garrulous but excellent jack-of-all trades, a real Mr Fixit, invited him to share a fried egg sandwich, which the man made in a miniature frying pan with the aid of a small calor gas burner. *And the tea, the hot sweet tea!*

He switched the engine on and pulled back onto the road. Traffic was scarce, and the car coasted down the steep slope, with the sea below and far beyond. Early morning mist swirled lazily upwards in the warming sunshine. Above it, a myriad of islands shimmered in the distance on his right. On reaching sea level, he turned the vehicle to follow the coastal road. Lost in reverie, the shuddering of the car as it rumbled across rough planking brought him back. With surprise, he realised he had reached the pontoons at Zadar. As the car bumped across it brought back the skin prickling sensation of earlier trips.

For no reason an image of the carnage on the steps of Queen's, Belfast flashed before him. It was beyond belief that Declan Rath, who, as a solitary gunman, annihilated their team, should now be his closest and only friend.

He dwelt on his feelings about his disfigurement. Two friends were dead and when he visited his sergeant in hospital, several weeks after the shooting, the sight of this family man, in total paralysis from the neck down, heightened his remorse of surviving. In a futile attempt, to alleviate his guilt, he believed the continued presence of the scars contributed to the price paid for the disastrous failure of the op. Surgery to repair his facial damage remained out of the question. Of late, however, he wondered if he was not being melodramatic. And to what end? The constant reminder, each morning, while he shaved did nothing to brighten the start of each day. He'd become accustomed to the shock others displayed on seeing him for the first time, and the aversion to the ruin of his features strangers could not hide. Maybe, back in London, he might—.

The rolling landscape before Trogir and the conurbation of Split appeared and faded behind him. Soon the terrain bordering the E65 took on a striking wildness as the road, clinging to the wall formed by the ragged jawbone of the Dinaric mountains, spiralled high above the sea. The skeletal remains of rusting wrecks and corroded chassis of vehicles littered the rocks below giving Spider warning. He shook his head to banish the drowsiness caused by the warmth and closed the sunroof before engaging the air conditioning. On reaching the end of the cliff-hugging segment he parked the car to stretch his legs. After a thirty-minute break it was time to continue.

With the turnoff for Gradec behind him, he passed the entry to the hidden port of Ploce and followed the road toward Metkovic. He decided against a final visit to town. Its charms, non-existent while he was there, would not have improved. The convoy members' old living quarters at Klek drifted by, and before long he reached the anomaly of the village of Neum, a hamlet with a five-star hotel. Once the epitome of modernity and comfort, huge chasms and fissures blighted its façade. It was a ruin; a grim, and expensive, reminder of the war. The damage to the deserted shell of a building, visible from the northern approach, remained unrepaired. The village, on a narrow strip of land, a salient only fifteen miles wide, overlooked a picturesque inlet, which provided Bosnia and Herzegovina's only access to the sea.

He passed through the Bosnian checkpoint without delay. On his termination he had not turned in his UNHCR private vehicle pass. He drove through the Zaton Doli crossing, back into Croatia twenty minutes later, again with no hindrances.

He had calculated that he would reach Dubrovnik just after seven that evening and drove the final thirty odd miles at a leisurely speed. From the tree shaded car park, he strolled to the booking office. There was space available on the overnight to Bari.

With four and a half hours in hand, he meandered through the old town spending his remaining kunas. Croatia's currency was not popular in the country; the D-mark, followed by dollars, was the favourite exchange and even sterling, going through a bad patch on the exchange market, was more acceptable.

He found a restaurant with tables and chairs on the sidewalk. With his postprandial espresso, accompanied by a Sambuca, he wondered how Rath was faring in *das Vaterland* and whether he'd have difficulty in locating his friend Siobhan.

There were few passengers on the ferry and, drowsy he retired to bed early. Only to find he couldn't sleep. There was a consistent hum of the ship's diesel engines and a dull pulsating pounding, insistent and hypnotic, but paradoxically not sleep inducing. Finally, when he gave up trying, he began to slip away. His last conscious thought was of his early days in his hometown.

◆◆◆

John Webb had married on his return from the war and lived with his bride at his parents' home in Sudbury. After several jobs in a short period, he left London to settle in Vange, later incorporated into Basildon, a new town some forty miles distant, created to house the overspill from the metropolis.

Within a year, the Webb's had a child.

Michael Norman Webb was a chubby, happy infant who chuckled and chortled but rarely cried. He was quick to crawl, and Mrs Webb found it difficult to catch him when he accelerated into top gear, small limbs pumping like pistons, to race across the kitchen floor. He was slow to walk and content to avoid the risk associated with verticality. Both parents disagreed as to his first spoken words; his mother believed them to be 'ball. Oh!' while his father swore, he heard 'bollocks', an epithet he used many times.

Primary and secondary school passed with few incidents. He was not bullied as his physical strength and aptitude for contact sports ensured his membership of the playground mafia. While at Laindon High Road he helped found a teenage gang calling themselves the Bazzers.

Soon afterwards he would meet the boy, who when he grew up would, through his avarice and inveterate criminality, endanger his life.

The gang, an odd assortment of youthful misfits, prepared to initiate its latest recruit, a wannabee member desperate for inclusion. Skinny and acned, he was nicknamed 'Swindle'. The venue for the test was the Woolworth Store in the High Street. The ritual would be basic but larcenous. It consisted of the theft of several items from the open display areas of the store's counters, and a successful exit. The items did not have to be valuable; their relocation from the shop to the gang's turf was adequate.

Spider and two other Bazzers waited across the road from Woolworth's for Swindle to exit. Fifteen minutes passed before he stepped out of the store. He saw them and waved his clasped hands in a victory salute above his head just as a large woman, wearing the standard Woolworth maroon coverall, exited and grabbed his upraised arm from behind. The surprised reaction of their newbie would have been hilarious had it not been for two policemen walking down that side of the street.

The tearful Cheatham had his pullover hoisted and several packets of plastic oddities removed from his underpants. The boys followed at a distance as the police led him away.

Three hours later, after booking and charging, a tearful and feeble attempt at bravado did not convince Spider, the only gang member who waited, that Swindle possessed the mettle to be a Bazzer. To his surprise, later that week, several of the gang members opined he had done enough to warrant entry to the gang. The caution he received for that day's larceny was to be the first of many 'accolades' that Swindle received over the next few years.

Due to common sense and maturity, which came early to Spider, he had left the Baz Boys before thievery blighted his life. Swindle remained in the gang and gained the respect of his cohorts as his criminality increased. He and Spider pursued separate ways but still met on occasion. On one of these occasions they found themselves in the same reception area applying for jobs as trainee mechanics at the busiest repair shop in town. To Spider's amazement, and more so to Cheatham's, they were hired.

◆◆◆

The first sign that trouble was on the horizon was when various hand tools disappeared. Each mechanic had his own tool board, a largish blackboard with the outline of specific tools painted in white. The two trainees shared one. The conditions of employment stipulated the worker be responsible for the equipment and to pay for any loss.

Their board had no deficiencies.

Confined not only to equipment, the pilfering continued. Some of the mechanics complained of cigarettes, small change and on one occasion, sandwiches going missing. Since no similar incidents occurred prior to the youths being taken on it was not long before they became the suspects. An impromptu search by a foreman located several of the tools in Cheatham's locker. Within minutes of Cheatham's long walk to the manager's office they called for Spider. To his surprise, Swindle had blamed him for stealing the tools. Cheatham tearfully explained, he had only stored them at Spider's request. A brief and acerbic dressing down by the garage manager ended with them being told to wait in the changing room until the police arrived.

As soon as they entered the room and before Spider could ask Cheatham blubbed that he was sorry, he had panicked, he hadn't meant to say what he did, he thought Spider wouldn't mind, as he had an unblemished record. But Spider noticed that Cheatham had a vein of determination when his co-worker refused to withdraw or alter his story.

They arrived in the magistrate's court, uncomfortably suited, and represented by the same solicitor. He recommended that Spider, with no previous, pled guilty and Cheatham with several previous strikes against him, did not.

Things did not go well for Spider. He was three months older than Swindle and considered by the magistrate to be the one who should have exercised greater maturity and ensured the younger defendant stayed on the straight and narrow. The choice for Spider was Borstal or the Army.

Swindle walked.

◆◆◆

Next day, Spider lay awake, warm and lethargic, listening to the caterwauling of gulls. Soon, aware of a pervading smell of ship's fuel he dressed and climbed on deck. In the bright morning light, the vessel was manoeuvring into position alongside the dock in Bari harbour.

Clearance through customs was uneventful and soon he was on the northbound autostrada. Several hours passed and it was darkening when he reached the Brenner Pass. Ninety minutes later he stopped to overnight in a wayside pension. An early rise saw him making good progress toward Calais. He found an empty space on the Chunnel parking area and after paying what he thought was an exorbitant price for his journey through a hole in the ground to the UK, Spider returned to the car. It would be some time before they loaded. He leaned his head against the headrest, closed his eyes and drifted into dreamless sleep.

Chapter Eight

Cheatham, a risk-taking opportunist, was neither impulsive nor careless. He would weigh up the options, identify the downsides and the possible outcomes. Sometimes, with few known factors or, conversely, too many variables, he would chance his arm and go for broke. The arms deal had been one of those instances but, with hindsight, deceptive. It appeared a no-brainer, without threat, zero involvement traceable to him and ripe for great dividends. *Should have been a revolving door. Pass go, pick up £200, pass go, pick up £200, ad infinitum—until that lunatic of a Croatian colonel interfered.*

Absent-mindedly he scratched his armpit then put up his arm and sniffed. *Ripe. Impossible to get accommodation, even for a night. Every damned hotelier in Europe wanted your passport.* In Croatia, they retained the document overnight to give the police time to check on all guests from out of country. So, no possibility of accommodation, therefore no shower. Ergo pong!

Mrs Ovasco had cursed him off their doorstep when he tried to seek shelter there. Partners. Friends. *My arse! Not down to me the smuggling went tits up. Mind you, if Ovasco remained under lock and key, little wonder his wife's pissed!*

He frowned. Where could that evil bastard Colonel Paroski be? He'd made the arrest, dragging him by the collar into his car, then to the airport, intending to hold on to him while he dealt with some other commitment elsewhere. But unexpectedly had to release him. There was no room in the helicopter. The pilot refused adamantly to allow the additional unscheduled weight *Thank you, Lord!* But why no follow-up when Paroski got back? No complaints about remaining at liberty, but it remained a conundrum. Where was he now? How did Paroski get wise to the smuggling arrangement in the first place? Fingers touching the tender bridge of his nose prompted the memory of those hellish minutes in the maniac's car. It remained sensitive after that bone crunching elbow punch. *Arsehole*!

What the hell happened to his partners? Ovasco and Stösser? Both still in custody?

I'm free. Maybe, the only one. But why?

The helicopter gunship that carried Paroski away must have been heading into the war zone. Even to a layman in things military, the armaments mounted on the exterior of that beast looked excessive. Deepest, darkest, war-torn Bosnia was the only logical destination. *It never got back?* Perhaps, the Colonel stayed there? Or even M.I.A? 'Missing in action', would solve much of his dilemma and end the worry of incarceration in a Croatian gaol. But if the man was toast, then so was his confiscated passport, and more important, his cash. Irrevocably deep-sixed. *Paroski can roast in hell but losing my money? That's the pits.*

To add to the misery, the man worked in the Croatian Special Branch, Military Intelligence or something in Security. *Arrogant bastard.* Logic dictated that, as part of a structured organisation, he reported to superiors or shared information with colleagues. *Right? There'd be records, wouldn't there, to act on?* Strange, little evidence existed of that. No hunt, no increased police activity or checks.

The thought dawned. *It's possible he's a loner, or someone who holds his cards close to his chest.* Less than credible, and reminiscent of an indifferent movie plot where someone, knowing the whole story, keeps it to himself, gets topped, and the others must start again from scratch to solve the crime. Improbable, but maybe, that's what happened? If the colonel never got back from the front, there would be no follow-up action to re-arrest him. In addition, if Ovasco and Stösser *were* free then likely there was a lack of evidence? That depended on them saying nothing while in custody to implicate him. Another thought struck him. If the weapons had got through, then they owed him the balance of his money. But, aware of the calibre of his partners, he doubted Stösser or Ovasco would get in touch to pay him. *What would I have done in their shoes? Yeah, well not much hope there. So, move on.*

He shifted position on the bench. As he stared across the road at the British Consulate building, he tried to get his thoughts into order.

Why not go back to work for the UN? Resume as manager at the aid base? *Because Webb, who is not stupid, must by now have been aware of the weapons. He'll realise my involvement. Better to have levelled with him? Shared? Nah, too damned straitlaced for gun running. Even if he took a bung where would I get the money?*

Spider, a formidable, aloof character who, if disgruntled, was not averse to showing his displeasure with his fists. He chuckled without mirth. His former employee would not want the people at HQ thinking he'd been privy to the contraband deal. The probability? No report existed—at least not an official one. Webb would demand answers and expect them from *him*. The experience of the nasty elements of the brutish Paroski episode loomed large. Again.

He sighed.

Best to avoid such a confrontation.

Drivers were a loose-mouthed and garrulous lot, and without doubt, it would not be long before something leaked to the ruddy United Nations High Commissioner for Refugees.

Nah, returning to base? Not a choice.

He had kept his credit cards and, although he had gutted and closed the Croatian account, then lost the money appropriated by that damned Rambo, Paroski, he could access his UK one. The passport, and his money, which that asshole impounded, was gone forever.

An option did exist. People lost passports every day. A temporary issue should get him back to Blighty and he had no intention, of applying for another travel document. Ever.

Mind made up, he rose stiffly, looked both ways before crossing the road, and limped up to and through the gates of the British Consulate.

Chapter Nine

Before he embarked on what might be the most momentous scheme of his long career, to destroy any possibility of a peace process, he needed to clear the decks of all extraneous issues and settle the score with Calum's murderers. And others.

The crossing from Dublin had been rough. During the eight hours overnight, he had very little sleep, and when he did, he had not slept well. The bunk was tolerable, but the other occupant snored, intermittently but loudly, so that the anticipation waiting for the next outburst irritated Liam. As soon as the boat docked, he hailed a cab for Lime Street. On entering the station, he made for the public phone boxes.

Liam keyed in the number from the address block of the letter then listened as the phone rang and looked at his pencilled notes.

'Bonjour, this is the Headquarters of the United Nations High Commissioner for Refugees, Geneva. You have reached Human Resources. How may I help you?'

'Oh, good morning. My name is Rankin, Peter Rankin and I am calling from Emergency Services, Norwich in the UK. There has been an accident, a bad pileup, this morning, and one of the seriously injured has the name of an employee of your organisation as next of kin. We urgently need to trace and get in touch with him.'

'Do you know which country and the branch or department?'

'We have reason to believe he is in Croatia, working on a relief effort. His name is Cheatham, Roy Cheatham. He is English.'

'Thank you. Please hold.' He could hear a keyboard in operation before the woman came back on the line. 'I'm afraid he no longer works for UNHCR. He left our employ some time ago.'

'Do you have a telephone number or perhaps a forwarding address?'

'We do but...'

'I fully understand, but this is urgent for self-evident reasons. I can follow this up with an official hard copy request but as time is of the essence...'

'Well, I suppose I could let you have the telephone number of Cheatham's next of kin. Perhaps that would...,' the woman broke in.

'Mr Cheatham's brother is in a critical condition and if we can't reach him in time...' Liam successfully kept the irritation out of his voice, and it paid off.

'Very well, then. And if you could let me have an official written request after the fact it would be helpful.'

'No problem,' Liam lied. 'Excellent. Thank you very much. I appreciate your help.'

After scrawling the number and address on the pad he hung up.

◆◆◆

Cheatham climbed down, pulled out his bag and slamming the door, shouted his thanks to the driver, who was not going to use the services at Thurrock but would head up the M25 to London.

He heard the gears slot into place and the vehicle rolled out of the slip road down the ramp back onto the M25. He swung his bag over one shoulder and headed for the entrance.

With a mug of tea and cellophane wrapped sandwich, and little change from his tenner, he was heading from the till toward an empty place when a voice called,

'Swindle? It is Swindle, yeah?'

Cheatham grimaced and gritted his teeth before turning toward the source. He didn't recognise the individual sitting at a table on his own. But he immediately recognised the blue coveralls with the white lighting flash on the breast pocket. How long ago was it that he and Spider had worked at Rennie's? He brightened and put the tea and sandwich on the man's table and pulled out one of the empty chairs. He held out a hand.

'Sorry, but I don't think I...' The hand was ignored as the man put his mug of tea to his lips

'Nah, you wouldn't 'cos we've never spoke. I had just come to Rennie's garage, been there a week then you and Webb got canned. But I was sure that I recognised one of the Ali Baba's. So, how's it going?'

Before Cheatham could answer the man made his own observation,

'Not too well from the look of you. Look like shit, man.'

Cheatham cleared his throat.

'I've been travelling. Just got back from the other side and got a lift from Dover.'

The circumstances under which he and Webb had left the garage had not been ideal. He flushed self-consciously.

'Trying to get back to Basildon, now'

'Won't be a prob, Swin, I'm on me way back there.'

Despite the offer of the lift Cheatham wanted to smash the man's face in. He hadn't heard the hated nickname since his manual workdays. You didn't have to be a genius to figure out the connection, though. *Fuckin' crap play on Cheatham - Cheat 'em. Cheating Bastard – Swindler.*

It had started to drizzle as they walked toward a recovery vehicle with a Ford Escort suspended from behind. The journey home became strained, as Cheatham's method of getting there was assured, he became monosyllabic and unwilling to chat.

❖❖❖

Back in Basildon. Baz. His hometown. He couldn't remember how long he had been away but the meeting in the *Three Bells* with Spider Webb seemed like a previous life. Which it was, in a way, and how the mighty had fallen, he thought ruefully. Still, he had some things going for him and he still owned his mother's house which was convenient now he was penniless. No need for any major decisions, however, until he had rested up—recharged his batteries, so to speak. There would be time enough to get back into wheeling and dealing.

He set down his grip and pulled the key ring from his pocket. After looking up and down the street, force of habit, he pushed his way in, past the built-up layer of junk mail and other post on the hall floor. With a heaved sigh of relief, he made his way into the kitchen for a long-awaited mug of tea.

The next two days were taken up in doing all the things an expatriate had to do on return to the UK. He registered at the Job Centre, to turn the tap on for his benefits, let his mother's butcher know that although she had died, he was back in country and would like deliveries again. He let his local milkman and the Post Office know number 13 was occupied once more. On the evening of the second night home he had a craving for a beer and threw on a coat before setting out for his local.

❖❖❖

He had a vague impression he was being followed but couldn't be sure. The sensation was weird, to say the least. He looked round but he couldn't make out who, of the several people behind him, it was, but the feeling persisted. He gave a mental shrug and walked on to the *Three Bells*.

That's the second time I've caught him staring at me he thought as he watched the curly-haired man at the end of the bar nursing a whiskey. Cheatham never believed in being confrontational, and was not about to start now, which was just as well as the man set down his empty glass and made his way through the throng.

'Cheatham? Roy Cheatham from 13 Bentham Road?' he asked. Cheatham recognised the accent as one from Belfast. He nodded.

'You might've noticed me on your way here. I apologise but I had to be sure. Can I talk to you about your time in Croatia? Would you like another...?' He pointed at Cheatham's glass. Cheatham accepted the offer and asked for a pint of bitter.

'Are you from the Press?' he asked.

'No, not all,' said the man quietly. 'Far from it. No, my interest in your time in Croatia has to do with a young man you hired down there. Calum MacDermot. That ring a bell? What can you tell me about him and his accident?'

'Hold up a minute here. Before I say anything at all, just what is your specific interest in

MacDermot? Is this for insurance purposes? Liability investigation?'

The man's face hardened at the questions. The thin lips narrowed, and his eyes seemed to grow smaller. Any semblance of warmth disappeared. Cheatham became rapidly apprehensive.

'Liability, you say? Yeah, that would be exactly what this is all about. Responsibility. Determination of who's to be held accountable. Who's going to answer for Calum's death, that sort of thing?'

Cheatham's self-control ebbed rapidly. *Christ, this bastard is scary!* He would be the last person he'd want digging into his involvement. *Whoa! Wait a minute, there. Relax. What can anyone prove about my involvement?*

'If I were going to tell you anything, and I haven't decided yet, I wasn't even there. All I have is hearsay.'

'Let's get one thing straight, don't be a feckin' idjit. Calum was my brother and you will tell me how he died and who was responsible. I'm thinking maybe it wasn't you. You don't strike me as someone who would be upcountry amongst the shit and bullets--but you can point me in the right direction, which would be nice, so no one need get hurt.'

At the word 'hurt' Cheatham flinched then looked around the bar in desperation. He couldn't control the panic that set in. He realised he was pushing away from this Irishman's presence so vigorously that he could not ignore the pain in his spine against the chair. However, he was also aware that an opportunity for him existed here to settle a score and extricate himself from blame. He'd much rather see this villain on his way after Spider. It might just work. He licked his upper lip.

'Let me see what I can remember.

'The man in charge of the convoy was a guy called Webb. Ex-Army. There were a couple of lads from your neck of the woods if memory serves.'

'Describe them.'

'Well, Webb had this scar—'

'The Irish. Tell me what *they* looked like. Names?'

'Rath. Declan Rath is the one who springs to mind. Big fella with black hair. Looked like he could handle himself. Webb was not quite as big, but he was fit. He could—' Cheatham's attempt to direct the attention to Spider again was blocked by Liam interrupting.

'Rath. Just fuckin' Rath.'

'I can't help there. I not sure they stayed in Croatia or are back here. I could make inquiries for you.'

Despite the cold-eyed stare he hoped he might have scraped through. He couldn't be certain, because this face was one that it was difficult to read.

'Where d'ye think they would be now, Mr Cheatham?'

The question's tone and delivery was devoid of expression--and all the scarier for that. Cheatham swallowed and determined to give an honest answer.

'I'd say they were on their way back. They could stay down there and soldier on, but I think it unlikely.'

'And why would that be?'

'Well, because of the guns—' Cheatham broke off realising that he had mentioned what he promised himself he would never voice. The Irishman pounced on it immediately and his lips twitched in the semblance of a smile. Now, there was not a hope in hell that this guy would let him off the hook.

Liam left his chair and came around to sit beside him. Cheatham blanched and flooded with nausea. The Irishman had neither threatened him nor given any overt indication that he was in danger, but the former convoy manager had an exceptionally well-defined sensitivity of when he had drifted, or been swept, into harm's way. The touch of the stranger's hand on top of his confirmed all his fears.

'I think you should start from the beginning and tell me everything, leaving nothing out. I'll be judge of what's useful to me. Look, there is no necessity for this to be painful, unless, of course,' his lips tightened, 'you want it to?

Slowly at first but then with more confidence Cheatham truthfully related all that had happened in Croatia. He did not include mention of his own complicity.

'This arms man, Stusser—'

'Stösser,' corrected Cheatham.

Liam ignored him and continued, '—do you still have the means to contact him?'

Cheatham pulled a face but nodded.

'I don't think he'd be pleased to hear from me, but I guess we'd still be OK since his stuff probably got through, although,' he said as a fresh thought entered his head, 'maybe the Croats have still got him. I heard he was arrested about the time they came after me.'

'You think that's likely?'

'I honestly can't say, but it seemed like they had stopped looking for me, so it might have been the same for them.'

'Them?'

'Yeah, my partner, Ovasco also got collared. If he's out and about I can get in touch with him and then on to Stösser.'

'I'll need you to do that. Let's go back to your place.'

'Just a moment. There's no way —'

'Now,' gritted Liam between his teeth.

◆◆◆

With the information he had gleaned from Cheatham Liam was set to go to Germany and accomplish two tasks. One, he would visit Herr Stösser whose line of business provided him with an anonymous source for the material he would need and two, while in Germany, stop off in Frankfurt to get their version of the hunt for his brother.

The concourse at St Pancras International Station was not crowded. Liam leisurely cleared the checking-in procedure to board the train. He found his seat without difficulty and stowed his bag above his head before settling down to reflect on his intended actions.

There had been no problem in arranging to meet with Stösser and Cheatham proved helpful. Although the arms dealer had appeared cautious, he agreed to meet with Liam but only in Cologne. Liam had no problem with this condition, as he preferred a face to face meeting with those he would have to rely on at some stage.

The French countryside hurtled by. Before long the staid, sombre Belgian landscape provided the moving background. The smoothness of the ride was hypnotic in its effect and Liam lapsed into a shallow sleep awaking when the Eurostar pulled into the Gare du Midi. Despite the 'south' in the name the station was not in that part of Brussels but stemmed from the fact that the final destination on the line was originally the south of France. Liam smiled sourly *or so the brochure said.*

On stepping down from the train he heard the announcement for his connection to Cologne. His watch showed he had fifteen minutes to find the platform before the arrival of the train heading north.

He glanced around, spotting the bag snatcher before the African saw him. Liam looked for the man's accomplice as he knew they worked in pairs and caught sight of the backup player further down the platform. He watched the first man scan the length of the platform and halt his sweep as his eyes settled on him. He pretended not to notice that he was selected as the target. The play continued as a surreptitious nod was given to the support snatcher who then stepped off towards Liam but passed him and positioned himself several yards away down the platform in readiness to receive the snatched bag. The exit was past Liam, who knew he would head back in this direction to make his escape, after the handover.

Liam smiled. His bag, which he would have to relinquish his hold on for the scam to take place, contained one pair of clean underpants and socks, his toiletries and two second-hand paperbacks from the Salvation Army thrift shop. Nothing of value would be lost should the two Africans succeed. The money for his purchase was in the money belt.

The platform started to fill up.

He put the bag down then walked a few yards off to read the information board. The snatcher, as he moved up, leaned down to scoop the bag up effortlessly, and strode down towards the accomplice already heading in the reverse direction to make the switch.

Level and only two feet away Liam back-chopped the partner across the throat with the edge of his hand and swiftly retrieved the bag from the falling man's hands before switching his attention to the original snatcher. The man realised that Liam was not going to be a soft touch but, out of loyalty to his fallen comrade, made the effort to avenge him. He came up the platform diagonally from Liam but moving so that he always faced the Irishman. He ignored his companion, emitting gurgling sounds with both hands on his throat and writhing on the platform. The knife was hardly clear of his belt when Liam thrust his bag onto the blade driving it up to the hilt. He immediately released his hold on it and slammed his toecap into the man's shin. With a cry of pain as the heel of Liam's hand slammed upwards into the base of his nose he let go of the blade, and bag, sinking to his knees.

The train to Cologne pulled in and as Liam turned and moved towards it, he caught sight of an old lady, with a Pekingese dog in her arms, staring wide-eyed at him. He gave her a ferocious grin, picked up his bag, removed the knife and, after throwing it down beside his would-be assailant, mimed an accentuated hush with forefinger on his lips before boarding the train.

◆◆◆

The taxi dropped him at address in Ebertgasse as dusk was falling and the shadows of the lindens were lengthening. He paid the driver, refusing the offer of a receipt, and looked up at the building. There was a light on the third floor. He moved towards the door, pressed the bell for number eight and waited. A man's voice said,

'Ja?'

'It's MacDermot.'

There was no reply, but the buzzer was pressed immediately. He pushed open the door, checked the location board for Stösser's flat, and entered the lift. The elevator stopped on the third floor and he saw the flat number eight opposite. The door was ajar, and he put his head around it and called out,

'Herr Stösser?'

The room was empty, but he could see another entrance, also open, leading to a second room. A voice, in guttural tones, called,

'Please, Mr MacDermot. Do come in.'

He shut the door and crossed to the other room. The man came from behind the desk with an outstretched hand. Stösser was not a young man. His shoulders were stooped and his physique frail.

'Please, do sit down. Can I offer you something to drink? Ein cafe or perhaps something stronger?'

'Coffee would be fine. Thanks.'

The arms dealer turned to the small table at the wall and switched the electric kettle on. As he busied himself with the cups Liam sat down and used the pause to study the office. Sparsely but traditionally furnished, it appeared comfortable but not overly so. There was what appeared to be a print on the far wall and the toneless yellow wallpaper, reminiscent of stale mustard, did not bring light to the interior of the office. There were no photographs of family.

Stösser laid down the tray on a nest table in front of the sofa and took his place in the armchair opposite. As he poured from the Delft porcelain carafe he asked,

'You had no trouble finding this place, Mr MacDermot?'

'None at all.'

'Good. I've done quite a bit of business, much of it through third parties with your, eh, 'parent organisation' and I think we have been mutually satisfied with the results. Are you here on their behalf?'

'Yes,' Liam lied, complicitly glossing over Stösser's falsehood, as the IRA never needed to do business with individual arms dealers. They were amply provided for by Gaddafi, the eastern bloc states, mainly the Czechs, and the generosity of the Sons of Eire in the United States. He continued,

'The action we have in hand is extremely delicate and we cannot afford any leakage whatsoever. That is why I'm here in person.'

'Yes, yes, no problem. Perfectly understood. Well, let me see. What specific weapons do you want?'

'I don't want any weapons as such. My interest is to get a substantial amount of Semtex or its equivalent together with detonators. We're prepared to pay above the going rate for them.'

Stösser smiled crookedly but made no comment.

'I don't care if the consignment is structured in smaller amounts as long as I can have them together for assembly. Initially, I'd like one hundred to one fifty kilos or more, if possible.'

'Such an amount causes me no concern. My suppliers are well able to provide such a quantity at short notice. It might take a day, or two to collate. How quickly will you want delivery? I ask because I have Czech material and military C-4 on hand, both in substantial amounts that might suit your needs. I have, or can obtain, several other versions of what you've asked. Must it be Semtex?'

'I'm on a relatively short time scale with a cut off in ten days. My preference would be for Semtex since I have had experience in its use and have no doubts about its reliability.'

'Might I take the liberty to ask if you have a means of 'packaging'? Delivery in public? Safe detonation?'

Liam did not reply but waited for Stösser to enlarge on his question.

'I can have the device assembled and packaged. In a Samsonite suitcase, for instance, with a remote detonation system. You are aware of the cell phone trigger?'

Liam raised his eyebrows slightly and leaned forward as the suggestion took hold.

'Go on.'

'Devised by our friends in the Middle East. It supplanted the radio-controlled device. The charge you specify can be installed in such a case I've described. It can be assembled so that the cell phone mechanism is removable to insert the detonator, together with a sim card of your choice. Your delivery to the place of operation should be relatively easy. Normally my clients order two, at least, of this item. Either for other targets or to have a rehearsal.'

Liam looked thoughtful as the suggestion took hold.

'I should mention to avoid the risk of tracking by those you wouldn't want to be tracked by, and the risk of premature erroneous detonation by a wrong number the sure way is to have the sim card and the battery removed from the apparatus and installed at the very last moment.'

◆◆◆

Liam rose early next morning and caught the train to Frankfurt International Airport. He booked a flight to Belfast and was not pleased that the only flight that would fit in with his plans was a late morning flight to Gatwick then to Belfast. He would defer his visit to the Frankfurt cell until he returned to pick up his 'purchases'.

As soon as he landed, he called Reilly.

Reilly's garage was not the tidiest work area Liam had experienced but the man's skill with all things mechanical was legendary. In addition, he was more than sympathetic to the Cause, and he was tight lipped. He had prepared, by modifying to specification, many of the vehicles used by the IRA for special projects. His top alteration had been converting a Mazda 626 into a mobile sniper platform which had been used with a high degree of success by the South Armagh snipers. The firer lay prone in the specially adapted compartment and fired his weapon through the hole cut in the boot lid. Of special interest to Liam was the knowledge that Reilly was adamantly against the proposed peace process, having lost two relatives in the fight against British domination.

The garage owner came out of the small side office, wiping his hands with a bundle of cotton waste. Because of the oil still on his hands he offered his wrist to Liam's outstretched hand.

'It's coming on well, Liam.' he said nodding to the people carrier positioned over the inspection pit. 'The engine's been replaced, and you've got the extra poke you asked for. I've lowered the roof on the inside, so you've got the compartment, too. Have a look at this,' he said proudly pointing upwards at the back of the vehicle.

'That's armoured plating to protect the passengers and driver. Nifty, eh? Not obvious though, is it?'

Liam was impressed and made his pleasure clear to Reilly with a twisted smile.

'Can't wait to try it out, Reilly, you feckin' genius,' Liam laughed. It would be unlikely that he would need the bullet proof addition but why run the risk of upsetting an artist like Reilly whose services he might very well need in the future.

'Glad you're happy, Liam, always like to see a contented customer. Two thou not too steep for you?'

Liam pursed his lips and shook his head as he walked around the vehicle running his hands down the bodywork.

'Make it two and a half but I'll need it sooner than I said.'

'It needs that paint job we spoke about.' The artisan in Reilly hated rushed jobs but the sweetener diluted his love of perfection.

'Day after tomorrow, latest, I'm afraid.' Liam persisted.

'Where ye staying?'

'Ah don't worry about that Reilly; I'll be back in the day after tomorrow, in the morning. You'll have it dry and roadworthy by then I take it?'

'No problem. But if anyone asks you never had it from me. I would never cut corners—'

While he was still speaking Liam shook his hand then headed to his car.

Chapter Ten

Despite the severity of his headache the journey back to Germany with the van was not arduous. Liam tried to nap for the twenty or so minutes it took to cross with the Channel Tunnel train but had to give up as the train pulled into the Calais offloading point. In a matter of minutes, he was heading down the E5 toward Cologne which he reached quite comfortably, thanks to the Reilly's efforts with the souped-up engine, in just under two hours.

◆◆◆

He was not in the least tired when he arrived in Cologne.

The Satnav simplified the city route to Eberstrasse. Using the intercom at the front door he told Stösser he was there. He refused the German's offer to enter but replied that he would wait until he came down.

Within minutes Herr Stösser, clad in a dark green Loden overcoat and Tyrolean hat was climbing into MacDermot's vehicle. Liam smiled sourly at the incongruity of an arms dealer dressed as a middle-class German bank manager.

'We need to get to the autobahn heading south. Turn at the end of this street.'

Some forty-five minutes later they exited the autobahn on to a secondary road and before long were travelling through a pine forest. Liam switched on the headlights as dusk descended and the light faded. After twenty-minutes Stösser leaned forward and pointed,

'Look for a small road going left, almost a track —ja, dort! There, there that's it!' The vehicle slowed and turned where the lights illuminated an old firebreak. Several kilometres into the trees the arms dealer tapped Liam's forearm.

'We are here.'

A flat roofed concrete building in the centre of a clearing appeared pale grey illuminated as it was by the sparse moonlight that filtered down through the pine tops. Stösser switched on a torch he had pulled out from one of the copious pockets of his coat and led the way to the entrance of the blockhouse.

'Bitte,' he said holding out the torch for MacDermot to take. He selected the first of several keys. Liam directed the beam at the numerous heavy-duty padlocks on the door as Stösser began the process of disengaging each one. Inside he located and switched on the first of four LED Lantern torches mounted on the wall. As his eyes became accustomed to the brightness Liam hid his surprise at the quantity of material proficiently stacked in the relatively constricted space available. He had seen arm caches before but this one resembled a well-stocked warehouse. Pre-placed on the workbench in the centre were two large Samsonite cases. Stösser directed his attention to them and then opened one.

'Watch carefully Herr MacDermot and I will show how this is armed and then made safe.'

Both men carried a case to the van and Stösser helped, with a certain amount of heavily expelled breath and, with what Liam took to be German imprecations. He handed the cases to Liam to fit them into the interior hiding place. Liam closed the doors and walked back to the block house with Stösser. As he was switching off the lanterns the German said, over his shoulder,

'We will settle the account as soon as we get back? Yes?'

'No need,' replied Liam moving close and placing the Walther CCP's muzzle behind Stösser's right ear as the arms dealer flicked off the last light.

◆◆◆

Replacing the locks and securing the door took longer than Liam had expected but he was in no hurry. Once finished he pocketed the bunch of keys, returned to his vehicle, reversed and headed back to the main road.

Satisfied that all was rolling towards a satisfactory conclusion and without hitch, he experienced the first hint of fatigue. Strangely, he noted, his headache had not kicked in, but he needed sleep now. He would check into the *Gaststatte* on the

E35 on the outskirts of Cologne. One hour later he collected his key for the chalet, was soon undressed and in bed.

By eleven that morning he was in Frankfurt. He stopped in the coffee shop in Wittelsbacher Allee and, after ordering, phoned Siobhan Callan.

Chapter Eleven

He drove at high speed but with competence and didn't look away from the road when talking to her. Siobhan had no reservations about his driving skills and his ability to keep them safe in the car, but the air of menace that exuded from the man was overpowering. She admitted her Celtic temperament was influenced by intuition, and a vivid imagination, but the aura of evil that enveloped him was palpable. He had been one of the front-line warriors for the Cause and it took no stretch of imagination to see that he would be ruthless. And cruel.

She regretted not having devised some excuse to avoid returning to Ireland with him, but it was after committing herself that the doubts began to surface. He'd been plausible, and humorous, in Frankfurt. At first, she'd been surprised to find that Jimmy was uneasy about him too, but his suspicion entrenched her insecurity. Both agreed that things felt they were not what they seemed, but neither had anything to support the disquiet.

They had laughed when they compared him, to Boris Karloff, then McGuinness but the laughter had been strained. They needed each other for moral support, in his company. Now she was alone with him, and it wasn't comfortable.

Aware the danger was not sexual but unable to define her anxiety, she could not dismiss it. It proved increasingly difficult to control. She no sooner determined to be alert than she began to question her feelings. Being apprehensive, almost afraid, had stood her in good stead in the three operations she had participated in against the British, but in those instances the object of her fear was clear – incarceration, bullet wounds, and even death. This unease was more worrisome, as it niggled away at her calm. She looked sideways at him, noticed the small smile and wondered what he was thinking.

When he had arrived in Frankfurt, he had been amiable, and his knowledge of the protocols demonstrated his validity. He had been sent by Sean Diffin, he said, to examine their capability for an action in Belgium. He introduced himself as Joe Craven, Diffin's deputy and temporary security director. Siobhan knew Craven was the second in command but had never met or seen the man. He was, to her mind, proficient in his examination of their unit on the first day. The line of questioning took a different turn the following day.

'So, had you met Calum MacDermot before you were asked to watch him?' he had asked. On reflection, now, she realised that, this was the moment the disquiet originated. She remembered thinking *Why is this relevant?* She lit a cigarette, examining his face through the initial exhalation of smoke, before deciding to reply.

'I saw him for the first time here in Frankfurt,' she had said, 'None of us actually got to meet him. They wanted us to keep an eye on him, so we did.'

'And he'd left before Rath showed up?'

She nodded.

'Were you acquainted with *him* before he left to go after the boy?'

'Who, Declan? No, we met for the first time on that job.'

'Ah, Declan, is it? And you decided to sleep with him then?' She had been surprised at his effrontery but then it was apparent this was no idle conversation. It was an interrogation.

'Well, the decision wasn't exactly unilateral. Would have been difficult if it was,' she riposted to show she did not appreciate this intrusion. If he noticed her antagonism it did not show.

'Did he let you know what he was to do if he'd located Calum?' The use of the forename was not lost on her, but she could not determine what it meant.

'No. After he left, I didn't hear from him again although...' she could have bitten her tongue out when she saw his eyes narrow at her next remark, 'He did say he would be back.'

'To see you?'

'I got that impression, yes.'

'So, if he were coming back through here, he'd be coming alone, no one else in tow, no Calum?'

'I guess.'

There was a long silence before he eventually said,

'There are others who'll want to hear your story.'

◆◆◆

They were making good time on the autobahn and would arrive an hour before boarding for the night ferry started Outside Cologne Liam pulled into a services area. She used the *Gaststatte's* toilet facilities and wondered if she should continue with him. She fought down the impulse to run. Her common sense, *which will eventually be the death of me,* won out and she returned to the dining area. The *erbsen suppe* she ordered was with her coffee on the white linen cloth. He watched, deep in thought, as she sat down, but didn't speak.

Liam relished the thought of inflicting misery on Rath, preferably by degrees. He had known what form it would take but had decided when and how it should occur. But occur it would — and soon.

Expressionless, he watched, as she lifted the filter off the coffee cup and spooned two sugars into the liquid. He was aware, but in a purely impersonal and detached way, that she was an attractive woman. She was intelligent and disciplined, otherwise she wouldn't be heading up the movement's operation in Frankfurt. Important to him was the inescapable fact there was some chemistry between the Removal Man and her. Sexual chemistry, signifying feelings of a deeper nature, that he would use to implement his revenge.

Back in the car and despite the unease she experienced, Siobhan slowly drifted into a fitful sleep. She awoke as they joined the queue of cars waiting to board the ferry, and within twenty-five minutes they had driven into the depths of the ship. She tried to ignore the unsettling fumes of diesel and petrol they climbed the mental stairs taking them to the canteen and social area of the vessel. They emerged onto the open deck in front of the cafeteria.

The sky had darkened considerably. The wind was strengthening and varying direction in gusts, as could be seen from the white horse wave tops in the shelter of harbour. The journey to Eire, scheduled to be approximately seventeen and a half hours, was not going to be smooth. The weather forecast was decidedly unfavourable. Siobhan was sure he knew she was uneasy and felt threatened. She could not fault his behaviour toward her, he had been polite and courteous, but now it was noticeably not warm.

The Irish Ferries vessel made for the open sea. Immediately the swell took hold of the ship. Siobhan, not a competent sea traveller, struggled to maintain her equilibrium thrown into imbalance by the movement. She fought to keep the welling nausea at bay. Her hands and face were clammy, and her mouth filled with saliva. Each swallow hinted, strongly, that the bubbling contents of her stomach might erupt.

Liam appeared to be at his ease. She found this annoying; consequently, she was short with him when he asked if she would like another drink, although she accepted.

As he went to the bar she rose and made her way to the toilet unaware that Liam had decided her fate at that precise moment.

Leaning against the bar he looked round to ensure that Siobhan wasn't back. Almost nonchalantly, he took the ampule of Flunitrazepam and snapped it at the neck. He tipped the contents of the phial into one of the cups and stirred the coffee with the wooden spatula before going back to the table. Siobhan looked pale and wan on her return but accepted the drink and took a sip of the hot liquid. With difficulty she held the queasiness in check and persevered with the beverage. She finished as her light-headedness increased. She felt ghastly and it showed.

The increased pitch and roll of the ship aggravated the giddiness. She swallowed repeatedly. Liam suggested that, despite the bad weather conditions outside, she might find some relief from the fresh air on deck. She stood shakily to make her way across the tilting floor. He accompanied her, taking her arm to prevent her collapsing.

On the darkened deck, with the wind reaching gale force, Siobhan found the dizziness had not lessened. The uneasiness increased. He steered her into the relative shelter of one of the lifeboats where the wind was not so violent. She swallowed heavily but could not prevent the swell of vomit that flooded her throat and nasal passages. She turned seaward and retched over the rail somehow comforted by the warmth and weight of Liam's arm around her shoulders. Suddenly, crouching and with his forearm braced across the front of her lower legs, she was effortlessly upended, and was plunging through the spray into the murky depths.

Chapter Twelve

The platform was empty as Rath waited for his connecting train to Frankfurt. He dialled her number again. Without success. *Switched off.* Rath closed the phone and returned it to his pocket.

Not getting through was affecting his mood and knowing he was doing all of this without prior arrangement, or even checking if she still wanted to see him, did not help. He was annoyed that he was on his way to Frankfurt to see Siobhan and did not even have her address. They had made love, but in <u>his</u> room at the Ramada, and the only means he had of contacting her was the number she had left on his mobile. *Stupid.*

He dialled again. This time, a female voice speaking in German from a machine gave, what to him, was a brief but unintelligible communication. He tried again, hoping to decipher the meaning. He thought he deciphered *'abgestellt? Disconnected?'* With the number out of circulation, he could not contact her. He wanted to kick himself for his presumption that, after his stay in the former Yugoslavia, it would be easy to resume the relationship. Locked on to the system and, due to his own folly, he would be in Frankfurt on a fruitless endeavour.

As the train pulled in, he shouldered his Bergen and joined the small group of passengers jockeying for door positions in the still-moving carriages. The more he thought of seeing Siobhan the less confident he became. Then he had an idea.

He told the taxi driver to take him to *Zur Post*. When they had searched for Calum they learnt of his whereabouts while in that bar. He couldn't be sure if it had been one of Siobhan's haunts, but he was confident that Jimmy Rafferty, her associate, was a regular.

Still early afternoon it was not busy. Although the man behind bar was unknown to him, he recognised the morose middle-aged man seated at the end. *Martin? No, it's... Marcus!* He took a stool close by and waited for the barman to acknowledge his presence. When he ordered he nodded in Marcus' direction.

'Marcus was drinkst du?' asked the bartender.

Marcus raised his eyes from his glass and looked at Rath as the barman indicated him.

'Das gewohnliches.' He stared, out of focus, at Rath, who hoped the man spoke English.

'He'll have his usual, a white beer, *eines Weisses.*'

'And one for yourself,' Rath said to the barman.

With both beers before them and the bartender had topped up his own half-filled glass, each raised his glass in silent toast.

'You are visitor in Frankfurt?' asked the barman, in stilted English.

'Yes. A day or two at least. I'm looking for some friends who drink here.'

'*Selber wie lästes mal?*' Marcus asked as he fumbled with his cigarettes. At Rath's questioning air, the barman translated, 'Same as last time?'

Rath smiled and nodded.

'I'm hoping to meet up with Jimmy Rafferty. Little Irishman who comes here?'

The barman translated, and Marcus grunted a reply.

'I am new here, but Marcus says your friend comes here at night.'

Relieved, Rath swallowed the last inch of his beer and ordered another round.

◆◆◆

He moved next to a window overlooking the street. With an exaggerated wave Marcus had staggered out and the barman finished his shift, handing over to a middle-aged woman, who was the owner's wife. Content to wait, Rath nursed his drink. It darkened outside. He felt the draught as the door opened and closed. The bar filled up.

He saw Rafferty, as soon as the man entered. His hair could only be described as 'carrot red' and he would never pass unnoticed in a crowd. Rath half stood. Rafferty detected the movement then a moment later, recognition showed on his face. With hands and arms outstretched Rafferty caused Rath a moment of awkward embarrassment as he hugged the bigger man. He removed his anorak and draped it around the empty chair, before saying,

'Great to see ye, Big Man. Let me get a beer then we can catch up. Can ye manage another one? Course ye can, course ye can,' he rattled on as he took his wallet from his coat. Rath waited until Rafferty had seated himself and taken a draught of his drink before asking, 'So, how's things?'

'They're quiet enough now but fer a while there, it was hectic. Yer man from home was over to check everything. Asked a lot of questions, mind ye. I couldn't see the relevance of many of them, but he seemed satisfied with the answers.'

Rath nodded showing an interest that was not real. He allowed Rafferty centre stage until he could ask about Siobhan.

'Quite a few questions about ye and yer project in the Balkans. In fact, it seemed his focus, he kept us busy fer the two days he was here. Me and Siobhan, that is.'

Rath wanted to ask about Siobhan but the news about the visitor and the man's interest in him intrigued him.

'Who was he, did you say?'

'I didn't, because he never said who he was to me. I'm thinking I heard Siobhan mention something like Craven. His first name was Joe that I know. From what he told us he was from the Staff, ye know. The things he knew, and the questions asked, proved he was well up there.' Rafferty became more uneasy as he saw that his information was causing Rath to frown.

'To be fair, Siobhan had her misgivings about him. She accepted he was genuine, one of ours I mean, but wasn't convinced he was on the official business he claimed. There were too many questions about the fella McCullum, the one ye were after.'

'MacDermot,' Rath corrected him. 'Calum MacDermot. What did he look like?'

'That's another thing,' Rafferty frowned as he thought back, 'We both thought he was the spitting image of Martin, you know — McGuinness, gimlet stare and nary a smile. He looked like he'd be an unforgiving bastard if ye upset him. Or even if ye didn't!' he joked weakly.

Unease swept over Rath. He knew Joe Craven. He'd been present on a couple of occasions he had assignments from Sean Diffin. And he looked nothing like McGuinness. Could this be MacDermot? The Man from Armagh? He thought he may have been in the man's presence, on at least two previous occasions. Once, when tasked, in the presence of a masked individual, to run interference for a bomber with a mission to attack Aldergrove Airport. He suspected then that the balaclava was the bomber. The other instance occurred when the IRA's South Armagh's commander paid a flying visit to a safe house, he had sheltered in. From the upstairs bathroom window, he caught the briefest sight of the man's back as he crossed the pavement and got into a waiting car. He was sure Liam MacDermot had been the man on both occasions. The news of Calum's death, and its circumstances, had not pleased certain elements of the Command structure. Things were unravelling, if MacDermot's involvement were a given. What if he were acting in a private capacity?

'How long ago was he here?'

'It would be...' Rafferty looked ceiling-wards as he tried to remember, 'seven days ago, no, I lie, it was eight days ago because Siobhan packed in her job on the Wednesday, the day before they left.'

Rath halted his glass halfway to his mouth as the effect of Rafferty's remark struck home.

'They? They left ...?'

'Aye, yer man said, on his second day, that he had got notification that Siobhan was to come home for a debriefing relating to the whole business. She was to travel back with him.'

Intense disappointment drowned the feelings of anticipation he had. Siobhan would be back in Londonderry. The last place on earth he wanted to visit.

Chapter Thirteen

She plummeted with her screams blocked in her throat by the force of air that rushed past as she fell. The sudden descent to the dark grey waters was halted as she slammed into a water-logged pallet. Searing pain raged through the front of her face. Then, consciousness leaving her, she scrabbled feebly to hook her fingers around the open slats of the wooden platform. She pushed her hands through the gaps, turned them to lock them in place at the wrists before oblivion flooded her brain.

Dawn broke and the sky lightened in the East. The cloud mass, no longer compact and dense, was breaking up and hints of blue brightness and spikes of sunlight poked through. The sea swell had lessened although a stiff breeze scooped up splashes of saltwater and doused her back to consciousness. It was bitterly cold.

Her mouth dry and her breath sour she could taste the metallic tang of blood. Her left eye, its lashes meshed together, by mucous, left her sighted in one eye. That side of her face was gigantic and swollen gargoyle like. The undulation of the water, the long up and down, up and down rhyme brought back her earlier nausea. She dry-retched then lost consciousness once more.

◆◆◆

The navigator of Rimini International commercial helicopter saw the shape in the water when the pilot brought the bird down to twenty feet or so to impress the CEO's party with the patterns of water disturbance. He gripped the pilot's arm directing his attention to what looked like a body. While the passengers were engrossed with the dancing spray and concave ripples, the blades of the chopper eased into a hover allowing the aviator to confirm it was a human form on the pallet. He was able to land, and although the aircraft was fitted with floats, it did not make for a steady platform. As the co-pilot and two male passengers pulled her aboard the helicopter, she groaned then spewed out gouts of water.

'Make for Blankenberg. It's the nearest landfall,' said the co pilot to the aviator after receiving the Chief Executive's instructions. The airman gave a thumbs up and the chopper swooped across the grey water beachward.

◆◆◆

Siobhan came to, wondering where she was. Strong sunlight streamed through the large window causing her to turn away from the glare. The shaft of pain caused by movement forced a sharp intake of breath. She winced at the stab in her chest, which in turn, incurred more distress in her lower face. Her hand touched the wired splints on her jaw.

At that moment, a nun entered and, seeing her discomfort, hurried from the doorway to the bedside.

'Please, don't try to move too much. The doctor wants to be told when you awake.' She operated her radio mike and called for the doctor. 'Are you thirsty?'

The nurse's English was excellent and accentless, but Siobhan had difficulty in understanding, as her brain seemed several beats behind. She forced herself to focus, attempted and failed, to sit up. The sister helped her into a sitting position and plumped the pillows behind her. Settled, she reached for the proffered glass and straw.

She finished the water as the doctor came in. She asked,

'How are you? Sore, I expect?'

Siobhan tried to purse her lips and sigh but failed miserably. 'I'll live,' she muttered.

'Ah-ha! Engelse. Wat heb ik gesagt?' she smiled at the nurse. 'Although you have no identification, I betted that you were English.' She took Siobhan's wrist and checked her pulse. The nurse, moving her hair aside, placed a thermometer into her ear. After seconds, she removed it, then nodded to the doctor.

'Well, other than a broken nose, a chipped cheekbone, fractured jaw and four broken ribs, you are in fine form. You'll recover quick and Mr Renoir's paid for your stay here.' At Siobhan's querying expression, she explained. "Mr Renoir's helicopter was flying over that piece of the water when they spotted you and brought you here. I should imagine he or one of his people will be calling in here to see how you are, sometime soon.'

She motioned the nun to one side and said a few words quietly to her, smiled at Siobhan, then left.

'The doctor thinks you'll be here for three or four days at the most. You'll be discharged when there is someone to escort you home. Oh, I think the police will also want to speak to you about the accident. Do you want us to notify the British Consulate?'

Siobhan stared at the nurse as though she hadn't understood, then shook her head slowly. Her mind was in a tumult. What should she reveal? What should she not explain? If the police back home interrogated you, a simple refusal to answer was the standard policy. Liam tried to murder her, but he was IRA, and so was she. This was not a matter for the police, of any country. She'd need at least appear forthcoming with the Consulate person, because she needed documents to pass Customs, but she would prevaricate. For the police interview, she made up her mind that she would say she had no recollection— of anything.

◆◆◆

She watched the gendarmes gather up their kepis and the sergeant return his notebook to his tunic pocket. They nodded cordially and left. Towards the end of their conversation, she had been aware of their frustration and she could sense that they wanted the matter closed as much as she did. It might not be so easy with someone from the consulate. On reflection, it might be easier if she claimed to be from the south and out of their jurisdiction. That, however, might be retrograde. Getting home as quickly and without fuss might not be possible if she involved another consulate.

Her ribs were still strapped up, but her facial dressings were more compact and neater. She did not resemble one of the walking wounded. Her few toiletries, purchased by Rimini Industries, lay in her lap. She had written the president of the firm expressing her thanks and left the letter with the ward nurse for posting. Her journey home was arranged by the British Consulate and Rimini Industries together. She had refused the offer of passage in one of the firm's aircraft. Much as she wanted to, she could not turn down the PR man's request to allow them to publicise the rescue and Rimini's largesse in her case. This could prove dangerous if the story broke internationally but she could not refuse to give something in return for her rescue. She had sent her uncle a telegram asking him to meet her at the Dover terminal.

◆◆◆

An attendant pushed the wheelchair to the rear of the ambulance. She stood unsteadily and allowed the escort to help her up into the vehicle's interior. From the leather armchair she leaned forward to wave at the nurse who had looked after her. The doors closed, and the vehicle edged out from the hospital car park onto the road to the harbour and ferry.

In response to the telegram, her uncle was there to meet her at Dover and, after several minutes of fussing, she got into his car and they set off on the English stage of the journey to the North.

On the crossing the thoughts swirled in her head. Why had he tried to murder her? Was it official? What had she done? She couldn't tell anyone else until she found out if it had been sanctioned or not. And even then? Now, her Uncle was asking what had happened that she had to be rescued. And she couldn't tell him. Daren't tell him. He looked sideways at her as he drove and saw that she would remain silent.

Her thoughts steadied and dread filled her. Back in Derry where could she be safe?

Chapter Fourteen

From the gloom of the unlit room, the woman gazed down through rimless lenses at Lambeth Bridge. Her pale blue eyes appeared unfocused. The evening streams of traffic and pedestrians, flowing across the bridge and swirling around the central island below, with flotsam of shiny roofs and wet umbrellas, did not register. Absorbed in thought, her mood was grey as the gauze of drizzle blurring the scene below.
Should one pay obeisance to political masters when asked to pursue dubious ends? The concept of loyalty, for most politicians is one of feudal fealty. They are ignorant of constancy as a two-way conduit. Blinkered and unequivocal support, for the political expediency of ministers with limited tenure, could never be moral and acceptable. The current gaggle are likely to lose their scrape nests at the next election, but this proposed change of law would have a substantial downside for the nation.
She sighed. *The tenet of just following orders has long since lost currency.*

As a civil servant at the apex of her career, this question of sycophantic support bothered her, or rather determination of the answer did.

Daughter of a G.P. and a nurse, whose career was cut short by marriage, Caroline Jones would not have envisaged becoming Director General of MI5 and ensconced in this Grade II listed building, when growing up in the Midlands. The founder of the Service, Sir Vernon George Kell would turn in his grave at the prospect of a 'gal' occupying his position in the organisation he founded.

She smiled.

Met his sole criterion for a woman, though; I have 'good legs'. Well, at least she did, when she worked behind a desk in Curzon Street. The thought brought back unpleasant memories of the ploys she adopted to sidestep the advances of predatory males and the frequency of the occasions when she acted vacuous and dim, tacitly unaware of sexual harassment. An overt refusal would have thwarted any possibility of promotion, if the man held a supervisory capacity

Despite her honour's degree from St Andrews, her present position would have been beyond her wildest dreams. As a raw novice, entering the Civil Service, though not short on ambition, her expectations did not rise to holding elevated posts in any line of work, let alone this one. Mores, custom and regulations discriminated against women; even more disadvantageous and restrictive for wives. The recollection of the constant injustice, blatant prejudice and antipathy in the tortuous climb brought on a frown.

Despite each handicap, with equal opportunity in the workplace to all intent atrophied, she continued to move upwards. Persistence, integrity, hard work, and often sheer bloody-mindedness, maintaining the inching upward motion, brought her here. It had not been easy with a predominance of the males in her chosen profession, who did not disguise their disquiet at her existence, even now, as Head of M15.

Her rise through the echelons of colleagues became an achievement that defied belittlement. With perseverance she triumphed in every department — counterespionage, countersubversion and counter-terrorism. She confronted all her challenges and overcame them.

Now, everything associated with that success stood at the brink.

That morning, as the others left the Cabinet Office Briefing Room A, described by broadsheets and tabloids alike as COBRA, Joshua Powers, Chief of Staff at Number 10, asked her to stay. The sight of his erect and ragged hair style, together with the cultivated three-day beard, grated on her sensibilities of tradition. The open necked shirt, a style worn by his leader and slavishly adopted by his younger subordinates, brayed pseudo working class. Eton was not renowned for alumni from terraced back to back housing.

He was forthright, rare for him, notorious as he was for relaying opaque instructions that were refutable and represented as something else should his master's interest predicate denial.

The P.M. demanded more in the way of positive support from M15, he said, and the organisation must be active in its backing of the Government's stance. Number 10's overuse of activity alerts, and the high volume of control orders in force, had not sharpened but dulled the public's awareness of the terrorist threat. With the support of the tabloids Her Majesty's Opposition found it easy to criticise these policies. Leadership's credibility sank to an all-time low.

She never disguised her views on protracted suspension of *habeas corpus* and spoke out against proposals to extend the time to detain terrorist suspects. The proposed strategies for prolonged pre-trial incarceration in the Bill were impractical. Complete invulnerability, a fallacy in any country, put civil liberties at risk. She recognised her obligation to give cogent advice to the Prime Minister on matters of national security. At the meeting, she re-iterated her apprehensions.

In vain.

Powers demanded a situation: a terrorist plot, a conspiracy assured success because of the inadequacy of time permitted to hold any suspected participants. An ideal scenario would be one, where the terrorists failed, but by the most minute of margins. It should be spectacular to ensnare the public's attention and more relevant the support of the Press.

He stared with icy hostility and did not respond when she inquired, with a raised eyebrow, 'Manufactured?'

◆◆◆

Handled with finesse, she mused, this fresh information Dennison brought forward might be a solution – providing more than expected. Her lips made a slight moue at the prospect; it might well be more efficacious than *they* preferred.

She swung around to face the men, the head of Northern Ireland Counter Intelligence (NICT) and his young PA, a shy but bright young intern, on fast track. Her slim fingers flipped open the dossier on the blotter. It contained sparse intelligence. She frowned, then looking up, said,

'In effect, we have no idea who he is?'

'Correct, ma'am,' replied the younger of the two.

Dennison was allowing his student his head.

'This name's a pseudonym? Noone?'

'A former handler in the FRU, that's the...'

'Force Research Unit. Thank you, Rutledge.'

'— gave it before we picked him up as an asset. It's 'No one'.'

He bowed over the folder in his lap and, sensing rather than seeing her disdain, his flush deepened.

'We haven't identified him?'

'Right. He's refused to meet. For long periods we hear nothing. Then, he re-appears, rejecting any reward which might help to get a handle — to find out who he is. He made all his earlier calls from public phones. He avoids a regular point of contact. The first time he surfaced, he gave the FRU gen on an arms consignment from Omnipol, which we relayed to the Dutch since it would pass through Holland.'

'But, as he wouldn't come in, and in those days, having no way of verifying his reliability, they remained loath to trust him. By the time we took him over, validating his information became easier by comparing it with input from our other assets.'

'You mean other agents confirmed his information?'

'Yes, ma'am!'

'Has he been useful? The material? Of value?' continued the D.G.

'Yes.' Rutledge murmured. 'He has continued to stay at arm's length, though. His last three messages have been on disposable phones, burners, where he uses each instrument for one call only.'

'He's Provisional IRA?' she asked.

'Well, no, we can't be certain. The results of the analyses on the calls show he is not a young man. We suspect he is from Belfast or in its vicinity. The speech patterns and word usage don't predicate a schooled individual but show a keen intelligence. The profilers say it's likely he's not a social person, pragmatic, with no genuine belief in causes or faith in politics. If a believer, he's now a disillusioned follower.'

'Or leader?'

'True, yes. The quality of what he's shared pointed to a senior position in the Provos. Data relayed by us allowed the French Navy to intercept the MV Eksund with the weapons from Libya, is one instance. Of late, he's provided insider knowledge on the Real IRA which might hint at a change of allegiance.'

'The Eksund? A little before your time with us, I would imagine? 86? What do you see as his motivation for supplying information, given his aversion for reward?'

Dennison leaned forward in his chair and spoke for the first time.

'The most reliable impetus— dissatisfied, disgruntled, unhappy for whatever reason, wishing it finished. He may be war-weary and ready to accept that it might, should, end any day now. The furnishing of material over several years shows his disillusionment. He has no incentive. It is not a recent manifestation.'

'Except he didn't walk in and he continues as somewhat of an enigma. The crucial question is — can we trust him?'

The D.G. tapped the dossier then flicked her hand toward the younger man in a gesture of dismissal. 'Thank you,' she said, 'Comprehensive and useful brief. Well done.'

The junior officer rose, reached over to pick up the file but the dismissive fingers waved him away, again.

'What Rutledge omitted to mention is that the informant claims this one will be worse than October 84.'

'A reference to the Grand Hotel bombing? Brighton?'

Dennison nodded.

She stared at the man before leaning forward.

'For reasons I won't go into here, I want no heavy-handed action to foil or neutralize this attempt, if it exists. We have two priorities. One, to identify our informant and two, most important, to get corroboration or the certainty it is a damp squib. Then go from there. Is the threat real? How imminent is the action? Confirmed or denied damn soon. Identify, locate, interrogate. Verification is all important. But I don't want it rolled up. Just observe.

Once we have a clearer picture, we'll give these miscreants rope, sufficient slack, until it's time to choke them. Don't use our in-house resources for this. Draw on the locker fund and make sure we have plausible denial.'

Dennison returned her stare.

'Yes,' she offered, 'but as it develops, you'll see why. Trust me on this.'

Back in his own office, chin resting on his linked fingers, Dennison examined the database of 'sub-contractors'. *Not an extensive list.* Many of these assets, true and tried, prompted a sliver of doubt that it's operatives may not react, in the short time scale he suspected available. He realised that the body of information would not produce what he needed. He closed the laptop.

As the thought entered his head, they needed a stroke of inordinate good luck, the phone rang.

Chapter Fifteen

As the phone rang Declan stepped away from the window and moved to the desk.
'Webb & Rath.'
'I'd like to speak to Mr Webb, please,' the caller opened. 'He called me earlier.'
'He's not available now but I'm Rath, his partner. Can I help?'
'I particularly wanted to discuss an issue in more depth with Mr Webb in person. Have you any idea when he'd be available?'
'I expect sometime this afternoon, possibly a little after two.'
'Could you tell him that George Dennison called back and has more information for him and will ring about two thirty? Tell him it is important.'
'Of course. I'll pass that on, Mr Dennison.'

◆◆◆

Things appeared to be going well for their budding enterprise. In the short time that Spider had been back in the UK, while he had been swanning around in Germany, the ex SAS trooper had made good use of his network of contacts and singlehandedly brought home a small but lucrative contract with the MOD. Good fortune had been with them because although the period between the time of award and the required start of the project had been minimal Spider was able to hit the ground running. It hadn't hurt that the Contracting Officer was a former member of his old Regiment. On his return to the UK Rath had taken some of the strain off his partner and helped to complete the undertaking. That had finished a short time earlier and now it appeared another opportunity was knocking at their door.

◆◆◆

Dennison replaced the receiver and looked thoughtfully at Rutledge.

'That was Rath. How does he connect with Webb? What do we have on him?'

'Other than the summary from archives? Not a lot. We started to build a dossier on him before the Macaulay murder at Queen's but to be frank, it was mostly supposition. Nothing hard and fast. Then the moratoriums and cease fires together with the emphasis on Muslim radicals pushed him and the rest onto the back burner.'

'So now he is over here and working with Webb in a commercial capacity?'

'And doing very well it would seem. The MOD used them for the Digby Project and said they were satisfied. Those two worked together in Croatia on the aid convoys. Seemed strange knowing their backgrounds; Webb ex SAS and Rath, allegedly one of the IRA's top executioners.'

'Murderers,' interjected Dennison.

'Sorry? Oh, yes, murderers. Rath must have had a reason for going down to the Balkans but I shouldn't think it was 'official' business since he worked for UNHCR while he was down there. Unless, of course, the circumstances changed?'

'Original job completed, perhaps?' suggested Dennison.

'We don't think he was there for an arms deal. There's a possibility he might have a connection with the death of Calum MacDermot, one of their spear carriers. This Calum had a claim to fame, in that he is, or was—'

'Liam MacDermot's brother?'

'Yes. He was killed in some sort of traffic accident, according to UNHCR.'

'The brother of the mysterious, shadowy MacDermot of whom we hold next to nothing?'

'Yes, sir. An intriguing aspect to all this is Collins' report.'

On seeing Dennison's raised eyebrow Rutledge explained,

'Our man in UNHCR, who says the last convoy those two worked on carried contraband arms. That's never been confirmed, we couldn't get a denial or confirmation from the Bosnians.'

'Find out whether Rath is still IRA.'

'Will do, sir. I think his 'prior' in the IRA might be an advantage provided he is no longer active.'

Dennison nodded. He started to read the contents of a folder indicating that the conversation had ended. Rutledge remained in the room. Looking up Dennison said,

'Something else?'

'There is. The RUC have shared that a Diffin has been under investigation for child abuse, specifically his daughter.'

'Not the Chief of Staff of the IRA?'

'No sir, but almost as good, it's his younger brother. He's been involved in community good works, helping with troubled youths and charities.'

'Fitting the stereotype for most paedophiles,' interjected Dennison.

'There's nothing conclusive enough for the N.I. ministry sanctioning a prosecution. None of it is common knowledge although the RUC thought we might use what they have as leverage. On the intelligence side.'

'Blackmail the IRA's Chief of Staff?'

'It is worth considering, Sir. We've subverted senior members, but this would be the pinnacle.'

'Give me a draft on how it would play.'

Rutledge nodded and made his way to the door.

'And Rutledge, before the end of today.'

◆◆◆

Spider Webb, CEO of Webb & Declan Associates, parked the Audi, and walked to the lifts still mulling over Rath's call about Dennison, who was no stranger to him. They had not been in touch for years. In fact, he had been a young SAS trooper under his command in the UK. Then the Falklands intervened, and he was to put his training to good use. In action the man had been outstanding and had proved exceptional in strategical and brilliant in tactical planning. Pebble Island was where it all came together

Captain George Dennison was the commander of D Squadron, the contingent of SAS despatched to the Falkland Islands. He had passed selection and became a member of the SAS within two years of leaving Sandhurst. As an officer his tenure with the Regiment would not be permanent unlike that of Spider's as a non-commissioned soldier. However, Dennison, as second in command, was quickly accepted by the men and in a short time had lost the somewhat derogatory epithet of 'Rupert' assigned to all young officers. Three weeks prior to the unit's despatch to the southern hemisphere he was promoted acting captain and appointed squadron commander.

Spider was a young trooper with three months service in the Regiment and was still on probation and under 'watch'. He was the youngest of the sixty-five members of the squadron.

Due to his inexperience at the time Spider was not one of the advance groups of SAS ferried into the Falklands by helicopter at night to observe the enemy's dispositions and communications. His first participation in action would be the night raid on Pebble Island during May 82. He would be part of a forty-two strong party to attack the airstrip that had been commandeered by the Argentinians.

◆◆◆

'Settle down,' said Dennison as he prepared to brief the raiding party. A map of the Falklands and one of an island yet to be identified had been taped to a makeshift display board.

'In twenty-four hours, we'll embark on HMS Hermes to our jump off point. Due to the presence of civilians in the vicinity an airstrike won't be used to neutralise what is now our target. It is an Argie airstrip. They have Pucaras and Mentor 34s both of which are used for reconnaissance and ground attack.

'We'll be there for thirty minutes max before we pull out. In that time, we will destroy the deployed aircraft, radar site, ground crew and the force protection garrison before we exfil by helicopter back to HMS Hermes.'

Pre-raid reconnaissance had been carried out by personnel from the Boat Troop of D Squadron, who two days earlier conducted an infiltration using Klepper canoes. They reported to Dennison that prevailing strong headwinds would lengthen the time needed to fly in from the Hermes and would therefore curtail the ninety minutes previously allotted to the offensive.

Mountain Troop was tasked with the destruction of the Argentinian aircraft, while the remaining personnel acted as a protection force, securing approaches to the airstrip, and forming an operational reserve. Spider was in the protection element. Each man in addition to his own weapon and ammunition carried two mortar bombs. One of the men from the reconnaissance party acted as guide. The troop assigned to the demolition of the aircraft laid the charges in an identical part of each aircraft so that they could not be readily repaired by cannibalisation of parts.

Spider's group stood by to open fire as soon as the explosives were in place. With rockets and small arms, they opened fire on the aircraft. This was the cue for the naval support vessel HMS Glamorgan to commence firing on the ammunition dump and fuel stores with high explosive shells.

Due to the brief available time the defenders, who until that stage had not responded to the attacking force, were spared an all-out onslaught by the SAS. The Argentinians response was desultory and did not prevent the raiding party re-grouping and preparing to move out. During the returning fire Spider was one of the two casualties on the British side.

The SAS were safely picked up again by the helicopters and returned to the Hermes. When the ship's medical officer treated him, he was told that the wound to his calf was caused by shrapnel from hits on the fuel dump by the Glamorgan's guns and not enemy fire. Spider's injury, though not totally incapacitating, ruled out his taking part in most of what was left of the conflict.in the Falklands

Shortly after cessation of hostilities. and their return to England Dennison's tour of duty with the unit at Hereford ended. He returned to his light infantry unit in the Midlands. In the ensuing timeframe Spider had moved up through the ranks and was a sergeant by the time Dennison reappeared for a second tour with the Regiment.

Within a month both were under orders, with four other troopers, to report to ETAP, The Airborne Troops School of the French military in Pau near the Pyrenees. They were to take part in combined development and exchange of methodology for High Altitude Low Opening (HALO) and High-Altitude High Opening (HAHO) that both armies were testing. These programmes were of special interest to Special Forces as another method of achieving covert insertion behind enemy lines.

In their free time they enjoyed the restaurants and culture of Pau. One of the troopers discovered a small brewery with a bar/restaurant in front in the residential area. The next night the rest of the SAS contingent accompanied him to the bistrot. Three paratroopers from the Groupement Commando Parachutiste (GCP) participants in the same parachuting trials were already there and invited the

SAS lads to join them. The Legionnaires intended to do some heavy drinking as the next day was Saturday. To forestall or delay the effect of the beer they were about to order a meal. Spider and his companions accepted and agreed to the recommendations of one of the Foreign Legion soldiers a tall, muscular individual of Nordic appearance. He turned out to be Irish.

Before long the conversation turned to experiences and tales of conflict where they were surprised at the number of actions in which the Legionnaires had been engaged.

By the end of the session sobriety had been banished but good behaviour still held sway. Over the period they spent in France a spirit of genuine camaraderie had developed between the two groups. Spider and Major Dennison agreed to stay in contact but especially with Del Kinnell from Portumna.

◆◆◆

As the lift took him to the third floor Spider hoped the renewed contact would have something to do with fresh business.

At his desk he called Dennison. The conversation was brief. The MI5 man sounded preoccupied and at his suggestion they agreed to meet at the Venetia, a small, secluded Italian restaurant in a narrow street off Essex Road in Islington.

With the dulcet tones of the Sat Nav to guide them Spider and Declan had no problem in finding the place, but parking proved more difficult. Consequently, when they arrived, Dennison and his assistant were already there, at a table in the back of the restaurant. Although bright and sunny outside, the interior of the eating place was subdued and dim.

The two men at the table rose. While greeting the newcomers Dennison signalled to the barman, who brought a bottle of Valpolicella, and stood by as handshakes and pleasantries were exchanged.

'Red ok?' Dennison asked. They all agreed, and the barman poured a measure into each glass. No one spoke until the barman had gone back to the bar where he busied himself polishing glasses.

'Do we need any menus?'

When the others shook their heads, the younger man, Rutledge, moved the cutlery away to make room for his briefcase. He removed four files and placed one in front of each man. Dennison leaned back in his chair.

'How have things been, Spider?'

'I can't complain. Took a while to get set up after Bosnia,' he laughed and exchanged a look with Rath, 'but Declan and I might just have a going concern now.'

'You did a good job for the MOD on that —'

'Digby,' Rutledge filled in.

'—project and now we've got some work for you. I won't BS you. It's hardly similar, but then the remuneration will be substantial. It won't be easy, could be dangerous,'

Spider held Dennison's look for several moments before asking:

'You've got resources enough for this sort of thing, so you've got to be approaching this from a hands-off position. You're employing outsiders and that means deniability. Right?'

At Rath's raised eyebrow Spider explained to him, 'Using subcontractors means they have the option of pleading not guilty if the proverbial hits the fan. They want someone who can get down and dirty on their behalf and of whose actions they can say they are absolutely ignorant.'

'Precisely. Would that be a problem?' queried Dennison.

Spider looked at Declan who shrugged.

'Negative. We're listening.'

'First there will be nothing illegal required of you, I can assure you of that, but we need, mainly because of political considerations, some wiggle room and all that entails.'

'Official Secrets Act parameters?'

'I'm afraid so, Spider, but I hope you would trust me enough to believe, that if you take this on, I'll provide any help I can unofficially, within the boundaries we establish up front.'

Spider indicated the folder in front of him,

Dennison nodded and watched as Spider and Declan opened the manila files. He was convinced from the body language and the ease in which they communicated that if there had been any previous enmity between the two there was no trace of it now. He wondered if there was any basis to the rumour that the two had clashed at Queen's when the lecturer had been shot.

◆◆◆

Spider pulled into the allotted parking space in the underground garage. Turning to Declan he asked,

'What do you think? Is it doable? For us, I mean?'

Declan frowned slightly.

'It's unlike anything we've — I've — ever done before. Basically, we're to find the proverbial needle. Something, we don't know what, which Dennison doesn't want to happen, is going to be done by someone, we don't know, who may be MacDermot may be not, sometime soon, but when, we don't know. It'll likely be destructive. On the plus side, from the info in here,' Declan held up the manila folder, 'we can be sure that the threat will originate from across the water, but it may not necessarily be Provo sponsored--although it's probably related in some way.'

Spider nodded and said,

'We're going to need access to information from sources that normally wouldn't be open to us. Cooperation. The RUC, Special Branch amongst others--can we take it as read that we'll have that? I'm assuming that is what Dennison meant by being helpful, as well as running interference for us? But, reading between the lines any help he gives will not be official and probably not agreed by his bosses.

'We'll likely have to spend some time over there as well.'

Declan nodded; his expression rueful.

'I won't be looking forward to that. Anyway, let's read this stuff separately, including the fine print, then discuss it.'

Both men climbed out of the car and, in silence, walked to the lifts.

'Have you noticed that the analyst who wrote this hasn't mentioned that this character Noone never actually gave them anything which involved bodily risk to any of the Volunteers? No possibility of stopping an action. Nothing they could act on. It looks like top grade but is never specific enough to move out on and stop.'

Webb nodded.

'So, why would anyone do that? Insurance, so that when he's rumbled, he could trade this off to avoid prosecution? Or is it taunting, like, the 'serial killer mocking the police' scenario? The bulk of the information was about material supplies and caches, handy for 'jarking' the weapons, but nothing timely about ops. I'm guessing he was a quartermaster.'

'Could it be a long-term ploy establishing a pattern of trust so he can perform a body-swerve and leave them checking out the wrong scenario as the real deal goes down?' Spider offered.

'We'll consider all these theories valid and eliminate or confirm them.'

Rath nodded as he pressed the button for the elevator.

◆◆◆

'How well were you acquainted with him?'

'Not at all. I'd seen him once but never saw his face. He was in his working clothes.'

At Spider's puzzled look, Rath couldn't help grinning.

'Balaclava.'

'MacDermot was far senior to me in the organisation. Whereas I was classified as a specialist, he was top echelon hierarchy. We didn't move in the same circles. Like many others I accepted his legendary reputation. I heard a lot, like many of us did, about his achievements in the field but nothing of the nature of the man himself. He existed as *the* bomber. The Man from Armagh. It didn't matter about indiscriminate killing only that the tally was high enough to register for the media. So, if I had known him, we wouldn't have got on.'

Both remained silent for several minutes then Spider asked,

'Tell me about his 'successes'.'

'Where to start? The problem is it is difficult to separate the myth from the reality. I think his first action in an ASU took place at Mullaghmore.'

'Mountbatten's assassination?'

'Yeah. IRA history also credits him as heavily involved in the planning of the Narrow Waters ambush.'

'Warrenpoint? 2 Para?'

'Yeah. He certainly got the acknowledgement for that among the rank and file. Two of the guys in the woods across the water engaging the British couldn't say enough about his dedication. Said they were inspired by the way his mind worked, especially his foresight to have the gatehouse, where the Paras took cover, wired to blow as soon as they set up there. Except—'

Rath grimaced. At Spider's raised eyebrow he continued,

'If involved in Mullaghmore, he would be about nineteen or twenty, so, it would be as participant not a planner. If that's right, he couldn't have had any active involvement at Narrow Water either since— '

'The same day,' finished Spider.

'And the two places are over a hundred miles apart. I think his legend started to be embroidered with myth when he became commander of South Armagh. It's reasonable to believe he was involved in the development and firing of the Barrack Busters. I heard of his involvement in their fabrication in South Armagh and their transport to London when they launched from the back of transit vans. In that attack on Number 10. And don't make that face about the busters, they were bloody good mortars, especially for home-made.'

'His speciality seems to be in blast and bangs. So, if he is orchestrating the op Dennison forecasts would it be that sort of thing? Big bang scenario?'

'More than feasible. Yeah, very likely.'

'Let's throw that around. See if we can come up with some situations under consideration by our new friend Liam'.

◆◆◆

'Not much happening here. Fancy a day out?'

'A day out where?'

'I've got to go down to see my Dad's solicitor about his will. That should only take about an hour max. Thought we could drive down and have a look around my old stomping grounds. Basildon. See if any of my old mates were back.'

'Mates? Who? Back from where?'

'Croatia. The one I had in mind was Roy Cheatham.'

'Gimme the keys. I'll drive.'

◆◆◆

Traffic on the M25 was medium to heavy but they made good time and arrived mid-morning.

'Take a right here. There's the pub. It's Cheatham's local, used to be mine. We'll have a pint and a sandwich then we'll see if we can find him.'

'It's still a few minutes early for them to be open. Let's just enjoy the peace and quiet.'

They sat in companionable silence for the next ten minutes listening to the muted tones of the radio. A traffic bulletin interrupted Classic FM as Rath stiffened and pointed to the entrance to the pub.

'No need to go looking. I'd recognise him anywhere.'

Cheatham continued across the carpark to door of The Three Bells.

'Give him five.' Rath nodded. They heard the traffic news out and as Wagner took over the airwaves, they switched the wireless off and climbed out of the vehicle.

The forlorn figure sat below the wall mounted TV. On seeing the cast on the man's arm, they looked at each other. Rath shrugged. Both stood in silence in the rear of Cheatham who was eating a sausage roll with his eyes fixed on the TV. He slowly became aware of a presence behind him. He stiffened then half-turned stiffly to look up. It took several seconds for it to register who was standing above him.

'Fuck.' He said succinctly.

'Good to see you, Roy, no, don't get up,' Spider said pressing down on Cheatham's shoulder so that he sank back down into his chair. 'We'll join you. Declan, I'll have a bitter. Thanks.'

'And how have you been, Swin?' he asked guilelessly using the derogatory epithet from their schooldays.

Cheatham gave a nervous grin in response and looked towards Rath at the bar.

'Fine. Can't grumble.' A silence ensued which was broken by Rath's return with the two beers.

Rath passed a beer to Spider and sat down at the table.

'What's happened to your arm?'

Cheatham's lower arm, which had been in his lap out of sight, was now on the table sheathed in plaster of Paris.

'One of your lot.'

'What? A dissatisfied convoy driver?'

'A fucking Irishman! Three days ago.'

'Why would 'one of my lot' do that?'

'Because I wouldn't answer his questions about you.'

This stopped Rath in his tracks and killed his smile immediately.

'What was he asking about me?'

'What wasn't he asking about you. Seemed to believe you had a hand in his brother being killed in Bosnia.'

'What did he say his name was?' asked Spider.

'MacDermot. Liam MacDermot,' answered Rath before Cheatham could reply. Turning back to Cheatham Spider said,

'So, you told him nothing and he broke your arm to get you to speak?'

'That's about it. He—' his reply faltered and died as he realised Spider was being sarcastic.

'Suppose we just have a quiet drink and you tell us what you told him, what he said to you, and what you agreed. And without missing out anything at all, Swin, we want the lot!'

◆◆◆

The conversation was sparse on the drive back to town as each was deep in his own thoughts. Spider broke the silence.

'So, this MacDermot. I'm guessing he was the brother of Calum? And, since he imagines you to be responsible, he suspects you were acting in some professional capacity?'

'Like I said we were in the movement together although we worked in different areas. He was first and foremost a bomber and I was a foot soldier.'

'But a specialised sort foot soldier?'

'You could say that. Look, we've never really spoken about what I used to do. Maybe, it would be better if I told you about my previous existence.'

Spider checked the mirror, made a gear change, flicked the indicator on to pull into the fast lane.

'Go for it,' he said.

Chapter Sixteen

The Captain announced the fasten seat belts requirement as the plane approached Belfast's International Airport, Aldergrove, named after a village lying to the west. Rath returned the magazine to the pocket of the seat in front and clicked the belt buckles in place. He would take a taxi to Belfast, some thirteen miles away, and meet up with Sean that afternoon.

He accepted that his experience and knowledge acquired in what felt like a previous life would be invaluable in the task ahead. He also agreed he was the most suitable choice to carry out this phase. But he had mixed feelings, primarily about returning to the province. He had no wish to stay in Northern Ireland any longer than was necessary and was uneasy about being here. The cease-fire agreements, concessions and their associated codicils had driven a coach and horses through the day to day criminal law of the Province but gave no idea how 'forgiving' they were intended to be. There were rumours of extensive amnesties but just how his own exploits would be viewed wasn't clear. He had confidence that MI5 would not pursue him now, but the RUC were a different kettle of fish and forgiveness had never been a trait. There were many in their ranks who had reason and justification to want him incarcerated or better dead. *For good reason. But it had been a war and both sides had often been extreme in the degree of brutality in their violence.* The past had been rife with informants and each branch of the Security Services had substantial lists of stooges prepared to lie. The RUC would have no problem in finding collaborative statements.

He rang Diffin saying he had landed. They agreed to meet in the bar of the Europa, suggested by Diffin, and both chuckled at the irony of the choice due to the number of times it had been chosen as a target for IRA bombs. Rath had decided that although he would trust Sean Diffin with his life, he would make no mention of the current project. To all intents and purposes this visit was personal.

A taxi was not difficult to flag, and he stepped out in front of the hotel sooner than he had expected. He saw Sean's grey head at the bar as he made his way through the throng of early evening drinkers from Belfast's burgeoning business community. Diffin gave a smile of recognition as he saw Rath and stood up with an outstretched hand.

'Welcome home, Declan. It's certainly good to see you fine and well.'

'I'm not sure I'm glad to be back but it is good to see yourself looking so fit. How are things?'

'Not so bad but first things first. What'll it be? The usual — Jamieson's, right?'

'I'll have a pint of the dark, please. It's a bit early for the good stuff.'

Diffin ordered the Guinness and as it was being poured took the opportunity to openly look Rath up and down.

'Aye, you're looking in top form, Declan, no doubt.' He picked up both drinks and moved away from the bar saying, 'I've another get-together later that won't give me as much pleasure as this one. Let's sit over there in the corner.'

Once seated Diffin leant forward and said, 'Well, tell me more about your trip. Not the sanitized version.'

'There is not a lot to tell. You'll know from the people themselves in Frankfurt that I went to Croatia to find MacDermot. It wasn't difficult. I made contact, but you hadn't told me that he got me out of Queens. I owed a lot to him. Not privy to that bit of background I was prepared to close him out if he refused to come back for questioning.'

'Declan, let that be for present, go on. What happened?'

'He was a driver for a relief supply convoy running gear up into Bosnia. When I found out what he had done for me I needed time to think and I signed on as well. On the run to Tuzla he bought it. His vehicle careened off the road, he was badly injured and didn't survive. I had no hand in it, thank God.'

'Aye, it's probably just as well he died as he did. I say that because one of our people on the inside has since confirmed it was young Calum who grassed, so he was guilty.' He took a sip of his whiskey and stared reflectively at Rath. 'Which made my relationship with his brother that more difficult. You remember how we had to pussy foot around because of Commandant MacDermot's position? I mentioned to you that there were some difficulties with South Armagh before you left? Well, they're almost sorted. The negotiations with the British have been developing in such a way there's a fair chance the War will be over soon. We don't want any hotheads or recalcitrant idjits taking unilateral actions that'll jeopardise any chance we've got of ending this.'

'The truce. Is it holding?'

'Well, that's what I'm talking about. We're not finding it easy holding some of the more reckless Fenians in check.'

'MacDermot.'

'Aye, the same. That issue was resolved. When the Council met last, the voting was close.' Diffin did not elaborate.

'But I'm not sure that he's going to go away quietly. He's planning a wrecking operation, made no secret of it. Action to prevent that will have to be considered. But you should be aware Calum's death will result in a feud and he will seek retribution on those he believes responsible for the boy's death.'

Rath nodded but looked troubled.

'And you'll be number one in his cross-sights before the rest of us.'

Again, Rath nodded, then placing his glass on the table, cleared his throat said,

'Do you know who is running the Frankfurt cell now?'

Diffin frowned slightly,

'You must have met her when you passed through? Pretty young thing but a great head on—hold up, are you asking why I think you are? Are you two an item?'

'Surprises me that phrase is still in use,' Rath tried to side-step. 'I went back to Germany after Croatia and stopped off. I wanted to see Siobhan, but she had left to come home. Sean, does MacDermot still have standing on the Staff?'

'No. He doesn't. Why?'

'I think he's been to Germany and asking about my assignment. Natural enough, I suppose, because of his brother's death. But whoever it was told them he was Joe Craven.'

'Joe? Can't have been. Doubt if he's even got a passport. I'll check though. I knew nothing of any of this. As far as I knew she was still out there. Are you going to see her? If it's up to date news you're after I'll get you a family number or a next of kin,' He opened his mobile and spent several minutes in conversation. During a pause in Diffin's call Rath said,

'She's back here or should be, they said out there. Called back for a debrief, I believe.

'News to me, Declan, but it's possible.' He returned to his phone call. 'Yeah, go on. When was that? Thanks.' He closed the phone.

'Give me your mobile and I'll put her uncle's number in there. Give him a bell and fix up a time to go see him. I can tell you; you'll get nothing over the phone.'

'There's something else I need to talk to you about, Sean.'

'Your retirement?'

As Rath expressed surprise, Diffin smiled slightly.

'Of course. It had to happen. Because of recent developments, it's hardly likely we'll have any more work for you. No, there's no problem there. It looks like they'll agree complete amnesty for our people, all of them. Even for the ones already serving time. I never thought it would happen, but we pushed for it against the odds and it does look as though they're going to buy it. If it comes off, you'll be well and truly in the clear. You've never been in their hands, have you? No, I didn't think so.'

'So, the myth is not true? In it until the end?'

'Well, it never was. If you can be trusted, you'd be free to go, provided we didn't need your services. We never wanted the myth to go away though; it worked in our favour over many years–it probably was true in the early days. No, it'll be fine, Rath.'

Rath raised his glass, reached out with it to touch Diffin's shot glass in a silent toast, and emptied it.

'Now, tell me what you're up to as a civilian? What have you been doing?'

'One of the guys on the Convoy suggested that when Croatia was behind us, we could try our hand at the security market.'

Diffin looked puzzled.

'The stock market? That kind of securities?'

Rath laughed out loud.

'No, the other kind of security. Checking out the need for safeguards within organisations, finding things or people for clients, and the like.'

Rath did not elaborate and didn't mention that his partner was a former SAS trooper. Nor did it seem pertinent, at this stage, to mention that on behalf of MI5 he also had a professional interest in Liam MacDermot.

They spent the next hour or so reminiscing and bringing each other up to date on the happenings in their lives. The drinks were replenished three times. As the light faded outside Diffin looked at his watch and smiled apologetically at Rath who nodded in understanding.

'Rath, before I go let me put something to you. With your previous skills and your new-found employment, you might be just the solution I've been looking for. We've mentioned MacDermot and how he might be a hindrance to everyone's future. Have you ever met him?'

'No, never. But, hold a minute Sean. If your meaning what I think you— '

'No, no way' Sean Diffin laughed. 'Would solve my conundrum but no. Would you be able to arrange surveillance of a sort? Track him to make sure he stays in his box?'

'I think that could be managed. I'd need to have more about him, photos, hangouts, where he lives--.'

'Of course. Let me link you up with O'Riordan. He'll get in touch with what you need. Let me have your mobile.'

Diffin keyed in O'Riordan's number and waited while the system put the call through.

'Rio, Sean. I'm on a friend's phone. He'll call later from this phone for you to collate some info for him. It's so he can follow-up on a job I've asked him to do.'

The conversation continued for a few moments as O'Riordan sought clarification. Diffin ended the call and passed the phone back to Rath.

'Mind, now, boy,' said Diffin in an exaggerated Irish accent, 'No feckin' memoirs!'

After a firm handshake they parted on the pavement and Rath leaned into Diffin's car and said, 'Thanks again, Sean. For everything.'

He turned and walked toward the taxi rank as Diffin drove away.

Seated against the upholstery of his taxi he reflected on his next move as they drove to his hotel. In his room he selected 9 for an outside number then called Spider with an update of what he had learned.

Chapter Seventeen

Watching from a table next to a pub window Liam saw Diffin lock his car, stop at the corner, and check both ways. Satisfied, he crossed to the entrance. He searched the room then, recognising Liam, crossed to the table. He pulled out a chair but did not sit. He held Liam's eyes with his own grey stare.

'What'll you have?' asked Liam.

'Guinness,' replied Diffin, removing his scarf and unbuttoning his overcoat. He sat down as Liam crossed to the bar. Taking off his glasses to clean them, he stared speculatively at the other's back. Liam brought the drinks to the table.

Both drank and, setting his glass down as he licked the excess foam from his lips, Diffin made a gesture signifying 'What now?'

'I need you to give me some information.'

Diffin's eyebrows rose but he remained silent.

Liam continued, 'What do you know about Calum and what happened to him? I heard that you'd sent someone after him, but I want to hear it from you?'

Diffin looked down at his glass and breathed deeply. 'I've already told you what actions we took and why. We would have kept you totally in the loop, but your expected reactions played a big part in it being kept under wraps. We had good reason to suspect that he had answers to questions about the Queen's op. An issue that has since been confirmed.'

Liam looked sceptical. To test whether Diffin was going to be truthful he asked what he already knew.

'How would Calum be involved in that fuck-up?'

'More than enough. As a getaway driver for extraction of our man, for starters. But then he took off for places foreign almost immediately after. Look, he was to get the shooter out and away from the area. For that he had the detailed timings, location, nature of the project. And of course, he did the job.

'The pair running the safe house knew some of the particulars. In fact, the woman did grass, but we realised that her input would be too late to set up that counter-op. That left Calum, and a big question mark.'

'And who he was related to had feck all to do with that conclusion?'

Sean Diffin sighed forcibly but ignored the question. 'By the time it was evident we needed to talk to him again he'd floated. So, we sent for him.'

'Who did you send?'

'Liam be reasonable. We had to be sure. The man was under orders to bring Calum home. No more, no less,' said Diffin as he returned Liam's unflinching stare.

'Who did you send?' repeated Liam.

'Rath. Declan Rath. He said he met up with Calum but didn't have time to get with him on the matter. Your brother, unfortunately, had an accident before that had a chance of happening—'

'Rath and accident? In the same fucking breath?' sneered Liam.

'He had nothing to gain by lying. He said Calum had bought it in a road accident and we have no reason to doubt it. We checked with your mother and she said the people down there wrote to tell her.' He toyed with his drink then looked away.

'I'm not happy with that. Where can I contact Rath?'

Diffin looked at Liam reflectively.

'Hold up with the questions. I've got a few of my own to ask you. Why can't you see the writing on the wall and support us in what are doing. We'll never get the British in a position like this again, where they are prepared to listen, and accept, our conditions.'

'Seriously, you ask me that?' Liam gritted quietly through tight lips. 'I wasn't hiding in Long Kesh under lock and key, playing the fuckin' Mandela, when it was the safest place to be with all the shit and shrapnel flying about outside. I invested my life in the struggle and won't abandon the value of sacrifices made because you want to play politics. I'm going to wreck, totally smash and destroy any vestige of success your negotiations might have. I intend to make it impossible for all of you to ever sit in the same building, never mind at the same table, with the enemy.'

Diffin sighed heavily. 'And how would you accomplish that, Liam.'

'By hitting those bastards so hard that Canary Wharf will look a damp squib and Brighton—'

Pushing back his chair and standing Diffin said,

'I'm going for a piss.'

◆◆◆

Liam watched the door swing closed behind Diffin and took the ampoule from his pocket. He snapped the neck and casually emptied the contents into the other's glass then poured some of his own Guinness into it.

Diffin checked the two cubicles in the lavatory then dialled a number on the burner. He spoke for several minutes then ended the call. He removed the back of the phone, extracted the sim card and flushed it down the toilet of one of the empty cubicles.

◆◆◆

He was swallowing a mouthful of the stout as Diffin returned.

'Well?' asked Liam.

'What?'

'I asked you about yer man Rath.'

'As far as I know he is in London. At least, that's where he called me from.'

'Diffin, don't be a shite. I want details and what you've told me so far won't hack it. Drink up and let's get down to specifics.'

As the conversation continued and more questions were put to him, Diffin found it difficult to focus on what was being said. It was not easy to collect his thoughts, marshal them into some sort of order and express them. Liam came around to his side of the table and sat down in the chair next to his. That made it even harder to concentrate on what the man was saying, and he gave up trying to turn to look at his questioner. His head became heavy. The pull of the tabletop was irresistible. His head fell forward, and Liam just managed to move the empty glass before his face made contact. Diffin's eyes remained open, glassy but blinking occasionally.

After a few minutes Liam pulled the almost comatose Diffin to his feet and supported his lax form. The pair made their way towards the door, Diffin's head lolling and his mouth open in stupor. Without turning his face to the bar Liam replied to the barman's offer of help by saying, 'I can manage, thanks. He'd drunk too many before he got here, silly bugger. I'll get him home.'

◆◆◆

On the darkened street Liam manhandled Diffin to his car. Liam parked the vehicle in the lane behind his mother's terraced house. Although Diffin was a much larger man he had no difficulty in extracting the semi-conscious and compliant body from the car and through the gateway to the back door of the house. Diffin had enough control of his body to remain vertical against the wall where he had been placed none too gently while Liam unlocked the door. Pushing it open Liam dragged Diffin by his collar into the hall, held him with one hand to open the cellar, positioned the slack jawed victim in the doorway then pushed him violently down the steps.

◆◆◆

Diffin, gagged and tied in the chair had, sometime during the night, soiled himself. He was badly bruised but not seriously injured from his fall into the cellar. This was not to last. Liam was pleased to see that the man was agitated and apprehensive. His own adrenalin increased as he detected fear emanating from Diffin.

Liam knew that he was different from other people in that his senses and emotions intensified at the thought of inflicting pain on another being. He convinced himself that he was not a sadist, for no other reason than such a person would appear to be controlled by his feelings and that, to Liam's mind, was weak, weak, weak. His enjoyment hinged on his ability to turn up or lower the volume of the victim's dread.

He lifted the metal shears from the work bench and came around to the front of the bound figure in the centre of the cellar. He placed the secateurs on the box in front of the anxious Diffin and walked around to sit on a chair behind him

'What d'ye know about interrogations, John? Did you ever do one? Ever been present when one was happening? No, didn't think so, too down and dirty for you. Well, that might prove an advantage— it all being virgin and fresh like. Unfortunately, being new, you'll probably miss all the nuances and won't notice where I'm different, and better I might say, than other interrogators you had working for you.

'All good interrogators have to enjoy their work, which means hurting people, some mentally, others physically. An example of mental torture and one of my best was when we caught that pair in the van from the Two Square Laundry scam. Remember? I didn't waste time on setting the stage for the questioning. I just up and shot the woman soldier right through the eye in front of the corporal. With not a scratch on him, we couldn't shut him up.

Despite the coolness of the cellar Diffin was sweating profusely. He licked his lips and said,

'Liam, please.'

'In any interrogation the secret for success is in inflicting pain, but more importantly--really effective—is making it clear to the interviewee nothing can stop the hurt other than an answer. Don't ever believe that bullshit about torture not working. Of course, people might lie initially to seek relief, but that is where the expert interrogator comes into his own, knowing what is genuine and what is not. It never fails, when the subject can't withstand the pain, and only the truth will halt the inevitability of more agony.'

Liam leant forward so that his chin was on Diffin's shoulder and his cheek was alongside the other's. Sean could feel MacDermot's breath on his face.

'Mind you, torture doesn't have to be out and out physical pain. The chief pillar of effective interrogation's eliminating doubt in the individual's mind about whether pain will happen. One main difference between me and any of the other good ones is that I believe in demonstrating serious hurt right up front. Before the curtain goes up, so to speak.

'See those bolt cutters? Of course, you can. You can't take your eyes off them. And you know I've hated you with a passion long before my forced retirement? So, there is no reason to suppose I'll go easy. '

He reached past his quarry to pick them up and return to his position. Diffin strained his neck to follow the shears.

'Out of ten, what marks would you give that for a detailed briefing? Ach well, never mind.'

He reached forward to touch Diffin's bound hands. The unfortunate recoiled and tried in vain to see over his shoulder.

'Despite all I've said it'll be interesting, for both of us, I'd imagine, if we discover that that you can withstand intense pain and tell me nothing.

Wouldn't that be a laugh, John? Anyway, let's find out, eh? Good, well let's get started. Ah, but where you ask? Tell you what, give me that forefinger—'

◆◆◆

Liam was about to tape the unresisting wrists together, saw the incongruity of the action and let them fall onto Diffin's lap. He checked the safety belt clasp was engaged then wrapped the assembly with another strip of the adhesive tape. Reaching over and around the unconscious figure he bound the man's neck to the safety belt. He removed five 9mm rounds from his pocket and palm fed them into the lax, open mouth then sealed the lips.

He threw the roll of insulating tape onto the back seat of the vehicle. From the boot of the car he removed a Tupperware box and took out the petrol-soaked rag he had doused earlier. Without closing the boot, he moved to the fuel tank, unscrewed the cap and fed the rag into the opening.

After a cursory look around the empty building site he lit the fabric.

◆◆◆

The small crowd and the three RUC policemen watched as the fire engine arrived and the firemen's heavy-duty extinguisher was turned on the blaze. It was patently apparent nothing could be done for the headless figure in the passenger seat.

◆◆◆

The meeting took place in the forensic officer's cramped office next to the morgue.

The men, one in the dark green RUC uniform of a County Inspector, came in from the autopsy room and untied their medical masks. They had looked on as the medical officer performed his autopsy on the mutilated corpse.

'So, what do we have so far? Do we know who it was?'

MI5's man on the ground in the Province, sitting on the corner of the forensic officer's desk, turned from the speaker and looked enquiringly at the medical man.

'Most of the skull was missing, having been blown apart. From the configuration of the empty cases and the damage caused it would appear the rounds, five nine millimetres, were in his mouth before the fire. I don't believe it was done with the intent of destroying the dental work to impede identification.'

The Special Branch representative nodded and said,

'Yes, no attempt to hide the victim's identity. The car number plate was left intact and the registration gave us Sean Diffin, who has been missing from his home for two days. He is, or was, a ranking Provo, formerly their head of intelligence who had moved up to number one.'

'If we needed more proof of who he was' the policeman put in, 'we found most of his fingers on the unburned part of the back seat of the vehicle.'

'If the prints are on file.'

'True. Anyway, they were removed while he was still alive. There's obviously quite a bit of hate in this.'

'That's putting it mildly. Any clues as to why?'

'None at all. All we've got is speculation.'

'So, speculate.'

'It's not beyond the bounds of probability that this is one part of a power struggle, but the vicious element in it belies that. I don't think this was a forced retirement from the organisation but rather some outsider with an agenda, and a bucketful of bitterness. It could even be the UVA, but doubtful. It might even be an attempt to hinder the peace process. Your man Sean was one of the major players. If it is, I'm thinking the PM will feel the hand of history round his throat and not on his shoulder.'

'Yeah, that well may be,' the MI5 representative bit the words off, 'let me have your report in writing ASAP. I'll need to get something off to London, and quickly. If their peace initiative has gone tits up there'll be hell to pay.'

◆◆◆

'Michael O'Riordan?'

'Yes. Rath? Declan Rath?'

'It is. Michael, I'm calling you about the things Sean Diffin said you could help me with. I needed some photos, for recognition purposes and details of known hangouts and any other info that'd help to locate a 'missing' person. The individual in question is someone Sean has concerns about. Are they ready?'

'Say no more, Declan,' Rio broke in sharply, 'The stuff will be here by the time you are. I'm still trying to get some updated headshots but it's unlikely they'll be available. They are, well, nearly, impossible to come by. He's a very shy character to be sure. Where d'ye want to meet?'

'I can come to yours. I've got the address.'

'Come through the back and I'll see you in the kitchen. The backyard door will be on the latch.'

Rath got out of the taxi at the post box and walked to the top of Clossie Street and across to the alley between the byelaw terraced houses. The rain earlier had left puddles among the missing cobbles in the alley and it was difficult to navigate his way down the lane without getting his feet wet. The very same cobbles would have been loaded into prams, wheeled up to the front line of the riot or disturbance and passed to the 'lobbers', the masked youths who confronted the forces trying to maintain law and order.

The door to O'Riordan's back yard was ajar, and he could see the seated figure of Sean's associate. He tapped briskly on one of the glass panes of the kitchen door before pushing it open and going in.

He clasped O'Riordan's hand.

'You've heard?'

Rath looked askance, 'Heard what?'

'Some bastard did for Sean. Fucking uncalled for vicious. Burnt. Maybe alive, in his car.'

Rath shocked and surprised dropped into the chair O'Riordan indicated.

'Drink?' Without waiting for a reply, he tilted the Jamieson bottle and poured generous measures into the two waiting glasses. Rath guessed O'Riordan was not pouring his first of that day.

'How did it happen?' Declan asked.

'There's not a lot of information yet. Sean got murdered, brutally, and his car torched with him inside. Hopefully, already dead. They're not releasing much information.'

'But you have your own ideas?' They touched glasses then drank.

'It's all connected with this stuff I got together for you, don't know how, only it is.' O'Riordan's slurred his words but he was not drunk.

'We'll be looking for him. We're going to get him. There'll not only be you looking for the bastard, but we'll be going balls to the wall to get him.'

Rath nodded silently. O'Riordan turned to the kitchen cabinet and got the manila envelope.

'Go through that lot while you're here. If you've got any questions, ask them when I get back. I'm going' for a piss.' O'Riordan cleared his throat and wiped his eyes with the back of his hand.

Rath spilled the contents of package on to the lino covered tabletop and spread them out; two foolscap pages of closely written longhand, several photos, all black and white and a page torn out of what appeared to be the Green Book. He cast his eyes over the details of a curriculum vitae for MacDermot. He'd study that more closely later. He returned the pages and the Green Book extract to the envelope and focused his attention on the photographs.

They showed the various stages of transition from youth to early manhood of a muscular broad-shouldered IRA volunteer. Rath noticed no recent takes. The definition of the subject was not ideal, and the lack of focus made it difficult to be sure that each photo pictured the same man. He heard a toilet flush, a door close and O'Riordan re-joined him at the table.

'These are all that are available? None more recent?'

'No, but I'm not surprised, are you? I'll bet you avoided cameras and photographers in the day. No freebies for the peelers. But then, I'm sure he's never been inside so they're unlikely to have anything on him. He's got no living relatives that we're aware of.

Here, let me see what you've got. This one, and this,' O'Riordan pulled two photos from the collection, 'these are the best likenesses. Just imagine a him little fuller in the face. The bastard!'

'He's responsible for what happened to Sean, you think?'

O'Riordan blinked rapidly and wiped his eyes.

'There's no doubt in my mind, whatsoever.'

◆◆◆

Rath phoned Spider and to let hm know he was flying back into the mainland and hoped to be able to brief him on what he had learnt.

Chapter Eighteen

She opened her eyes and lay motionless as she stared upwards from the pillows. She was awake, and she wasn't. An off-colour joke, about a wife examining the ceiling over the shoulder of her husband, while he performed, poorly, crossed her mind.

'Aye, this one too could well do with a paint job,' she smiled to herself.

She threw the duvet aside and immediately regretted the action as the pain burned across her ribs. After several, tentative, deep breaths, she eased her legs out of the bed and agonizingly pulled on the headboard to achieve a sitting position. Her feet searched and found her open slippers. Gingerly, she stretched to the bedside wooden chair and pulled the flannel dressing gown to her lap. A brief respite then she stood and put it on.

Three weeks had passed since her return to Derry and occupation of the flat her uncle had rented for her. Thank goodness he had, she thought, because she had been in no state to do so on when she got back. On a short-term lease of three months it would have to do until she was again in unfettered good health.

She put the duvet back in place to retain the warmth. The clock on the dresser showed 5.30am and it was still black outside although light was wanly making a brave attempt to broach the darkness. She filled and switched on the kettle. As it heated, she spooned coffee into a mug then looked out the window and up at the dark mass of the city wall in the middle distance. Born and bred in Derry she had only been up there once. That school trip seemed a lifetime ago. Nearly was, she thought, as the vision of the plunge through darkness into the slough of the English Channel made its first visit of the day. She halted her hand as she reached for the kettle and pre-empted the shudder that accompanied the mental image.

Back in bed with the hot drink, she drowsed then woke with a start to sip, then slowly slid back into nascent dreaming.

◆◆◆

Her first memories were of the Holy Child primary school and the mornings when she would leave home in the company of her older brother Kieran. He'd take her to the school gates before doubling back to begin his morning's work at Doughty's green grocers. For her, primary school was a happy time though no events stood out as being special; as a small girl her experiences lacked the awareness of life's realities and the memories of that time were warm, fuzzy and shapeless.

The first fully formed memories were of St Mary's School for Girls and each of these was tinged with sadness and bitterness. Despite the downside of familial tragedy, she did well in her studies and especially languages achieving a passable standard in French but excelling in German. The German poets proved to be the magnet. She loved the simplicity and concise nature of the language; her favourite was Salis-Seewis, who she had been surprised to discover was Swiss. She turned more and more to the poetry as life, with its shocks and losses, became at times unbearably real.

Kieran was no longer with the family having become involved with the Derry Citizens Defence Association and dead within three months of joining at 18. Her father had left them, and she remembered little of him, although she adored his younger brother who was then, as now, her favourite uncle. He had been so unlike many of the other males she knew. She had never heard him express a political view and he'd never commented, for one side or the other, on the day to day violent clashes with authority that occurred in the Province.

She, on the other hand, had been vociferous in her politics, even as a fourteen-year-old. Admittedly, she had no original thought but was partisan to the extreme in her support of the IRA. She attended every organised disturbance or riot and although it was mostly boys who threw the projectiles she had lit and thrown a petrol bomb at an RUC Saracen. Two bombs had been put together by her boyfriend and he had given her one to throw. The glass shattered, the fluid splashed all over the armoured plate, some even running down the visor into the body of the vehicle. Unfortunately, her beau turned out to be the only Catholic youth in the whole of Derry, an utterly useless nonce, who did not know that sugar added to the petrol was essential for a viable Molotov. She later learned that he had no pretensions in supporting the cause but thought impressing her would grant him sexual favours. Four months after that incident he was immolated when a rubber bullet brought him down before he could lob a lit, correctly constituted Molly.

One of her friends, whose brother laid claim to being one of the hard men on their estate, recommended her to him. He cleared it with Battalion who recruited her as a messenger and carrier for tasks over the weekends. She successfully completed several innocuous runs or missions, the only serious one, and the deadliest, was when she wheeled three grenades in the bottom of a baby's pram past a Brit checkpoint. The soldier, a youth not much older than she was, was naïve enough to think that no one would smuggle live weapons with a living baby shielding them.

This period in service with the IRA did not last long as she had managed to get an internship at The Journal. Although she was employed purely in a gopher capacity in the early stages, her work attitude was appreciated by her supervisory editor. After a few weeks, during a break one morning, she suggested an interview with some serving IRA members to give the paper's readers an insight into the whys and wherefores of the Struggle. Initially, not enamoured of the suggestion, he changed his opinion when he became aware that she was acquainted with some 'activists'.

He briefed her on what questions she should ask when it was clear that the interviewees would accept no other journalist. The meet was arranged and, the two she met and interviewed, wore the de rigueur balaclavas. One was a battalion commander. At the end of the session as she prepared to leave to get back to the paper, one of the minders, a tall well-built softly spoken masked figure with a southern accent invited her for a meal. She did not know why she refused.

Three days later as she was leaving work an attractive man wearing horn rimmed spectacles stepped in front of her and said,

'Well, a coffee, then, somewhere?' She stared at him for seconds before the accent registered and she realised who he was. She laughed out loud at the incongruity of it and the humour of his approach.

From her seat at the table she watched as he ordered and paid for the drinks. She tried to arrange her thoughts. His hair was a mass of curls, marginally long, and reaching his collar. From its sheen she could see it was clean. His shoulders were broad, and the beard made him look academic and simultaneously, a raffish pirate. True, he was several years older than she was but that added to the allure and his attractiveness. If he should ask, she would.

He did.

◆◆◆

After two weeks of intense togetherness, when her feelings for him continued to grow day by day, she moved in with him. As she collected her books and belongings her uncle tried to dissuade her but only briefly. He had always known if she had set her mind on a course of action persuasion did not work.

The house was on the far side of the Creggan and near the border with Donegal. He was continually surprising her with casual revelations. He told her that he hadn't been a bodyguard at the interview but was far more senior in the hierarchy and had been there to ensure no mention of ongoing operations occurred and to assess how valuable such interviews might be.

When he suggested that the organisation had a need for women of character in the fight for an independent Northern Ireland, she was thrilled not only at the offer but that he thought her a woman.

She was seventeen.

◆◆◆

After three actions as a fully-fledged member of an ASU that accomplished its objectives with clinical success, she noticed that his attitude and previous warmth toward her had cooled. There was still sex, but it became less frequent and he balked at physical contact, on the less frequent occasions when he was home, in a way that had not happened before. Morose and sullen he became offhand toward her. The first great love of her life was about to end.

She came home from the paper one afternoon to find him leafing through one of her German books. He asked if she spoke the language well and if she had ever been there. She had not and the subject closed. It was not mentioned for almost a month when she was given a new mission.

She arrived in Frankfurt with another IRA member Kevin Haines whom she had met for the first time at the briefing for the move to the major banking centre. She was to be Haines' assistant and liaison point between there and home while he set up a functional network among the expatriates. They shared a flat in Oberursel and to all outward appearances would be partners. The man's sexual preferences precluded any possibility of a relationship based on physical attraction. Kevin's tendencies toward pederasty was one of the reasons why he was not operational in Northern Ireland. The authorities were investigating his and the activities of others at a haven for waifs. His IRA affiliation was in danger of being uncovered. It was rumoured that MI5 had a connection in the running of the home, so a decision was made to send him to Germany.

As cover Siobhan got a job at the Contracting Centre for the U.S. Army in

Wittersbacher Allee while Kevin was hired by the Army's Class Six facility. They frequented the bars in the city in the evenings and in their free weekends mingled with numerous compatriots. Frankfurt, as well as other areas in Germany, where the Americans had depots or training areas, were boltholes for IRA members or sympathisers who moved to avoid interrogation or detention by the British. Many of them were employed by the U.S. Army in clerical capacities as they had English as a first language. Two of these, including Jimmy Rafferty, were co-opted into service and three other Irishmen were inducted.

What they were not aware of, until the trap was sprung, was MI6's working relationship with the BND, the Federal Intelligence Service. The BND located Haines and facilitated his 'transfer' to the UK, ostensibly justified, on the results of investigations into the happenings at the boys' home in Belfast.

By default, and despite her relative inexperience, Siobhan became the head of the Frankfurt faction. Although, actions on the continent by the IRA took place against the British Army in the northern part of the country they had been small-scale. The main thrust of her efforts that of quartermaster, maintaining communications, arranging weapon and munitions deliveries gave her a sense of contributing in a meaningful way. She had reasonable success over the two years she ran the cell then came the call from Derry to locate Calum MacDermot.

And Declan Rath came into her life.

Chapter Nineteen

There was an hour before his meeting with Siobhan. When her uncle suggested The Bogside Inn as a meeting place he had readily agreed. Afterwards, his natural caution kicked in and he reminded himself that not all his former comrades in arms would welcome him back in the heartlands.

From his vantage point on the City walls, with a clear view of the Bogside, Rath was ideally situated to see the movement of any individual in the panorama below. The whole of Westland Street as it rose in a steady incline toward its intersection with Lone Street was visible. This was Sunday and there was little movement, vehicular or pedestrian, along the length of the road. He had a nagging apprehension since he had been back in the province that he was far from safe. Although the RUC was a threat that couldn't be ignored, his erstwhile colleagues posed the greater danger. Conscious of what MacDermot intended he determined to be alert. A lapse of attention could prove fatal.

The Bogside pub, on his left as he looked down, was across from the house displaying, on its gable end, the mural of a child, schoolgirl Annette McGuigan. Another victim of mindless violence, ignited by the tinder of hate, on both sides, and ever liable to erupt into, raging, destructive conflagration.

    He lit a cigarette and looked to his right towards the Rossville Flats. Memories of January 30th, 1972 flooded back. It had been another Sunday like today but more memorable. As an adult, with hindsight and the maturity to revisit the milestones of his lifetime, the recollection still inflamed his emotions. The effect of the horrific events of that day had destroyed any semblance of a carefree teenage. He was eleven and would be plagued with frequent nightmares and bouts of bedwetting until his mid-teens.

◆◆◆

    Since the earliest hour of the day marchers from all over the Province had arrived at the starting point of Bishop's Field to take part. To all intents and purposes, it was to be, by Northern Ireland standards at least, a peaceful demonstration. The two arms of the IRA, the Provisionals and the Officials, agreed not to resort to violence, so nothing untoward was expected. A crisp but sunny winter's day developed as it progressed towards the departure time of three p.m. All marches were against the law, having been proscribed for several months, although the route was common knowledge. It would be marshalled by stewards. The route would progress through Southway, Brandywell and the Bogside on its way to a declared destination of the Guildhall. There was no intention of maintaining this goal and the real destination was to be Free Derry Corner where speakers would address the marchers. However, like all marches this one would take a circuitous route through the Catholic enclave before its end.

The surface atmosphere was serene but there was an underlying uneasy tension. The sky was clear and cloudless. What was to develop was totally unforeseen and tragically catastrophic.

It would be a massacre, raw, unadulterated murder; the summation of rash, inexcusable and unforgiveable action by the British State, committed in its name by their servants, the British Army. The soldiers had been bussed in from Belfast to Derry to deal with this un-authorised demonstration, a massed march they viewed as a confrontation. The subsequent killings, and wounding, had been birthed by the illogical, idiotic decision to use 1 Para as peacekeepers. What fool in the command structure of the British had decided to use the Parachute Regiment? Trained as they were for frontline close quarter action, armed with high velocity rifles, as reactive as Doberman Pinchers, they were unsuitable peacekeepers to control a Republican sponsored march of thousands. They were to be the 'snatch squad' or the arrest element of the controlling force. Their success in foraging into a crowd and bringing out whoever they targeted was well known. They operated with the cohesion of a wolf pack and viewed perceived threat as cause for retaliation and retribution. Other units had suffered at the hands of 'terrorists' who operated with, in their eyes, no standard of equitable professionalism or even decency. The Paras did not intend to be 'victims'. This made them less than appropriate for the constraint of a mixed bag, of men, women and children, on the move.

Prior to this march, eight days previously, Derry marchers had their first confrontation with 1 Para when they were baton charged and cudgelled off the beach as they marched toward the internment camp at Magilligan. On the 27th of that month two RUC personnel were ambushed and shot to death by the IRA in the Bogside and the previous day rioting and rock throwing had erupted in William Street. The junction of this street and Little James street was known as Aggro Corner. Each member of the security force's crowd control had to be apprehensive, not knowing if the IRA would maintain its promise of no involvement. The likelihood of petrol bombs, acid bombs or nail bombs was a constant in these 'peace' marches.

Any protest march was fraught with danger of violence and damage to person and property. But Irish protest marches were in a class of their own. None could ever be free of hotheads, belligerence, recklessness and impetuosity and a fair share of instigators. It was the nature of the Irish. Utter frustration, which had festered over the generations, was never far from the surface and when the boil burst it materialised as unadulterated hatred. It had to be recognised that for political ends much of this could be sparked off intentionally. By either side.

The British had shown they were past masters. It was common knowledge that when the Army first arrived in the Province, they were welcomed by the Catholic population, who believed they were there to prevent the imminent bloodbath threatened by the Protestant para militaries. When the Prods organised marches and riots against the police and the army they held all the cards. They controlled the programme of where and when. The soldiers on the ground had very little respite being constantly on standby. Until the British decided that a certain amount of 'prompting' could change the balance. One prime example of this was when a Marine Commando, whose unit was involved with stand-by duties to prevent violence erupting, at the opening of Ian Paisley's Free Presbyterian Church in Ravenhill. He lobbed a smoke grenade down the aisle, with the connivance of his superiors. The swarm of irate 'church going Christians' who streamed out of the church were arrested and a relatively quiet, and early, night was had by all. One incongruous aspect of the mainly Protestant unrest was that mobs never congregated when it rained.

The leaders of both factions of the IRA had stated that they would not be active during the march. However, and not made public, was the codicil that if circumstances or provocation provided an ideal opportunity of a worthwhile strike then The

Staff wanted the right players in place. In advance of the march the organisers co-opted members of the Official IRA to be crowd stewards. The Officials may also have placed gunmen, in the way the Provos did, to react if necessary. It was common knowledge that the Army would position snipers throughout the area in the close vicinity of the barriers they erected to kettle the marchers.

◆◆◆

The young Declan Rath was ignorant of all of this.

◆◆◆

With his foot in Jamie's hands and his own palms against the bricks a final heave from below allowed him to reach the top. He straddled the yard's wall and leaned down to pull the other boy up. Both swung over and hung down, searching for the stacked beer crates with their feet to shorten the drop to the ground. Once in the Blucher pub's back yard, they snatched the empties and filled the hessian sack. With difficulty, they helped each other climb back on the crates to negotiate the wall back onto the lane. They planned to hand in the bottles to the Grange pub at the bottom of Leckie Street and claim the deposits. They'd share the refunds and go to the pictures next day. And binge on sweets. To avoid spending the money on mundane things, like bus fares, they would walk into town.

Jamie had shown up shortly after midday and the boys started out for the 'flics'. They were both excited, resulting in pushing and shoving, short chases and fake, wildly imaginative kung Fu moves. Sometimes against each other sometimes against non-existent opponents along the length of Laburnum. All was accompanied by yelps and grunts in true Bruce Lee manner. By the time they reached Creggan Road the boisterous play had petered out and they were recounting plot lines and enthusing about stars of other films. The continuous hum, at first subdued but growing louder, passed unnoticed. Then, at William Road they met the column of marchers.

Both boys watched for several minutes before Jamie grabbed Declan's arm and rushed forward to join the column. Once in the flow they were swept along. They lost contact briefly and it was with difficulty and only by seizing hands that they were able to remain together. They had no idea which part of the crowd they had joined. The mood of the crowd was not peaceful and there was spitting, stone throwing, and shouted abuse at the soldiers observing the march's progress. There were individual confrontations where a marcher would go face to face with a soldier and pushing and shoving would take place but in general these would sputter out as the march pressed on and gathered up the wayward protester. The boys hooted when a woman lobbed an ice cream carton filled with human excrement at a trio of RUC members. They exaggerated grimaces of distaste as the odour of the diarrhoea filled the air when it splattered down the uniform front of one of the policemen.

The hubbub increased in volume into a shouted brouhaha as one section of the crowd encountered the first major cordon of the military units in the vicinity of Aggro Corner. These marchers, unfortunate or misguided, instead of following the main body turning right in the direction of Freedom Corner, continued forward, to confront the soldiers manning a barrier in William Street. There was shouted vilification and rock throwing by a large number, mostly youths. Scared but exhilarated, the boys, pushed to the side of the road by the forward surge of the incipient rioters, could only watch.

Just before 3pm they heard the first shot, quickly followed by three or four others. In frightened apprehension they stared with widened eyes at each other. They couldn't be sure from which direction they came. Years later Rath would have no doubt about who had fired those shots. They were undisputedly fired by the Army, as the resounding metallic thwack of .762 ammo was unmistakeable. But, at that moment in time, their anxiety froze all interest about who had fired. Instinctively they were aware Aggro Corner was not the place to be.

Pandemonium and panic reigned in the composite mind of the demonstrators as they fled from the sporadic bursts of fire from the troops. After two more short outbreaks of firing, directed at a breakaway element of marchers, it stopped. Galvanised into motion Declan punched Jamie in the arm and, closely followed by his friend, took off down Rossville.

The adult Rath understood fear, had experienced it more times than he cared to remember, but to be able to act in the face of terror or dread, self-control was essential to harness the adrenaline and get a result. That control did not come easily and required will-power to inhibit imagination and block out images of injury or death. It also required frequent practice to be able to maintain the pretence of cool-headed resolution.

The boys and the shocked marchers had no sense of purpose when the mass subconscious was viciously assaulted and torn apart by the high velocity bullets that ripped through their ranks. The firing started again as they reached the northern Glenfada Park flats. They ran to the barricade to join others sheltering behind a mound of rubble. One of the shots struck the stones and ricocheted in a high metallic scream. Rath and Jamie panicked even more and fled from comparative safety toward one of the blocks of the Rossville flats. As they took off three or four others at the obstacle also fled in the same direction. Suddenly, fifteen tons of armoured vehicle, travelling at speed, careened into the car park and swerved into a man and a woman behind the boys. The remnants of the group that had fled ran around a burnt-out van and joined several people, white-faced and stricken, sheltering in an alley off to the side of the open space. Soldiers exited from the rear of the vehicle and one, who looked like an officer, fired his rifle above their heads causing them to cower in futile defensive postures. As one the men, women and the two boys rushed in terror from the narrow lane.

In the next burst of fire Jamie was struck and fell. Rath crashed into his falling body and tumbled over him to land face-to-face. Declan, wide-eyed with fear, looked into the wide open, but unblinking stare of his lifeless friend. He struggled to his feet and blind with panic ran across the tarmac.

He saw a priest waving a bloodstained handkerchief as he led a group of crouching civilians out of an alley. Rath doubled across, and bending his knees, rounding his shoulders, joined the end of the group.

◆◆◆

A sudden movement below roused him from his reverie and brought him back.

He watched in surprise as she entered the bar in the company of what were clearly two paramilitary heavies. Her uncle must have connections but why were they necessary? There was something seriously out of kilter here. He walked down the slope and crossed the road to the pub.

The interior was dark due to the dim lighting. The pseudo mahogany woodwork contributed to the lack of light. There were empty tables in the vicinity of the entrance but three tables at the far end of the room were occupied, and he walked toward them.

Siobhan and the escorts were seated at a table on the mezzanine floor. She recognised him immediately. She did not seem overjoyed to see him but appeared apprehensive. She stood up. Her two companions looked in his direction then also got out of their chairs.

'Siobhan.' He smiled and leaned forward to kiss her cheek. She drew back, flinching from him, but smiled wanly.

Rath looked at the two men then at Siobhan. He heard the click of a shutter and snapped his head back to the smaller of the escorts who had just used a mobile phone to photograph him.

'In case we need to contact you again,' the man said in a mocking tone. They took their seats. Rath pulled over a chair from the next table and sat down. She edged away from any contact. He struggled to imagine what the cause of this diffidence might be. A niggling thought sprang to the fore. Was it fear and not a lack of confidence?

'Siobhan, what's wrong?' He asked this while looking at the two men opposite, both of whom returned his gaze with set faces. She looked sideways at him but didn't answer.

'I went to Frankfurt to see you only to be told by Jimmy that you'd left to come home. I thought that maybe we could get to see each other again—' He stopped then said, 'For Christ sakes, can't you two go to the bar and hold hands or piss off altogether?'

The older of the two held the lapel of his coat away from his chest to let Rath see the butt of a .38 Webley, held Rath's stare for a moment longer, then stood. He touched the shoulder of his companion who also got to his feet.

'We'll be out of earshot at the bar, Siobhan, but you'll be safe enough. You, however,' he leaned down toward Rath, 'stand a good chance of being put down.'

Surprise flashed across his face as Rath's right hand grabbed the lapel of his coat, pulled him down almost to the table while his left thrust inside the jacket to grasp the pistol. Rath did not withdraw his hand but they all heard the click as he cocked the weapon. With his hand still inside the man's coat Rath bit out the words.

'And you, a very good chance of being gelded.'

The other escort had not moved motivated either by slow reflexes or a wise head. Rath lowered the hammer under control and withdrew his hand.

'Siobhan. At the very least I deserve an explanation. Please.'

For several seconds she made no reply, then having made her mind up, nodded to the two guards who returned the silent gesture. The one who had been threatened straightened the front of his coat, turned and walked towards the bar. His companion followed.

Rath stood.

'I'm going to get a Bushmills. Would you like something?'

She shook her head but held his gaze, then looked away out of the window for what seemed to Rath to be several heartbeats, then having made her mind up she turned back and nodded

When he came back with two whiskeys, she said

'Sit down, Declan.' She moved to make space.

'I'm living a nightmare and have no idea what I've done to bring this horror down on me.'

Rath remained quiet and waited for her to continue.

'I've wracked my brains, but I don't have an inkling of why he would want to kill me.'

Rath instinctively knew she meant MacDermot but said nothing.

'I've told no one, no one, close to me,' her voice broke 'for fear of bringing it down on them and no one else in case it gets back to him and I'm considered a risk and it starts all over again.'

Pieces started to fall in place as Rath listened.

Siobhan's voice broke several times. When she finished, she smiled uncertainly.

Rath returned her smile.

'I can see why you were unsure of me. But it's beginning to take shape and it is connected to me.' She blinked in surprise, but he touched her wrist.

'Let me explain. Young MacDermot died in a road accident in Croatia. It was truly accidental. However, I was there under orders to bring him back for questioning or – because of this MacDermot is convinced that it was a termination with prejudice at my hands. It wasn't but with his mindset it would be difficult to convince him otherwise. So, through no fault of your own, you're in MacDermot's mad hatter vendetta. To get revenge for the death of his brother. And all down to me.'

'How can that be? What reason would he have to go after me?' Rath took out his cigarettes and leaned forward to light her's.

'He came after you because of our friendship. He tried to kill you to get back at me.'

'But, how would—? 'She flushed as she recalled that she had told MacDermot.

Rath thought for a moment.

'I won't lie, I went to Croatia with instructions to settle the young MacDermot issue …well, other things came to light that made the mission kind of complicated. Calum *did* die but from his injuries after losing control of his truck and going over a cliff. He hadn't been judged so—'

'I know how it goes, Rath, and lack of proof or a solid determination of guilt wasn't always —'

'If you believe nothing else, Siobhan, believe me, I had nothing to do with his death.' He took a deep breath. 'In all good conscience I couldn't. Not after I found out he saved my life.'

She took a sip of her drink and waited for him to continue.

'I'll tell you some other time but now I'm—'

'There's no hurry. I believe you and that's enough for me, for now. The rest can wait.'

◆◆◆

The barmaid watched, arms folded and squinting through her cigarette smoke as the big man stood, finished his drink and kissed the sitting woman on the cheek. After a glance at the two escorts crossing the floor towards him, he left her at the table, and walked out. A minute or two after the door closed behind him and with a leisurely look at the group of three, she reached for the phone, turned away from the solitary drinker at the bar and dialled a number.

◆◆◆

Glenda Gorman was known as the Bogside Snout. Despite the porcine appellation she was not an informant for the RUC or any of the other State forces. She was staunchly for The Boys, and although not a member of the IRA, she gathered a surprising amount of information on their behalf. She was the reservoir for the streams of gossip and rumour that flowed in the Brandywell ward. The provider of news of what transpired daily in the RUC station office where she worked as a cleaner, she was an inveterate collector. The detritus of wastepaper baskets, jotter pad indentations and the contents of the oft unsecured file cabinets were all grist for her mill. At weekends, when she didn't work, she circulated through the Bogside keeping an eye open for new faces and for those old faces that the Boys for some reason or other wanted a word with. She was proud of the work she did and was considered an invaluable asset by those who valued her information. To date, three men had been kneecapped and one possibly 'nutted' due to her input. The latter she couldn't be sure of, but the man hadn't shown his face since Glenda passed on the 'relevant', so it was feasible to assume he had become one of the disappeared. Probably, tucked away in the missionary position on top of some recently buried corpse planted in City Cemetery.

Many of the people who worked in the shops, pubs and markets, of the Creggan, Bogside and Brandywell knew of her unofficial function of earpiece for the Bogside IRA. Since she could also pass on reports of how supportive contributing individuals were, there was a constant flow of information. Glenda sieved through this for what she considered pertinent and mentally logged it for delivery to her paymasters.

As she waited for her turn in a chair at the Glowtop hairdressers her mobile vibrated. She laid the copy of Hello magazine aside and answered.

'Glen, Fiannula here. Got something for you.'

'Listening, Finn.'

'The big fella you said to keep an eye out for was in and has just left.'

'Goin' where?'

'Can't be sure. Wasn't in hearing range, but he passed the window going towards the town, along Lecky.'

'Thanks, Finn. I'll see ye right.'

'Hang on, Glen, he was drinking in here with the Callan woman from across the road — in the flats. There was two of the boys, looking like minders. I've seen one of them in here before. In here a few times, but I've not got his name. Can get it for you, though?'

'Nah, you're fine Finn. See you.'

She closed her phone and thought. There was not enough to pass on she realised, and it might not be the right 'Big Man'. But if it was Declan Rath Finn had clocked then it would be worth her while to make sure then pass that on. And if the Big Man had been giving attention to the Callan girl then it was odds on, he'd be back. Knowing when, was the tricky part, but not impossible. It would require 24-hour surveillance on the apartment block and, of course, on the woman. None of this would be a problem. That's why a woman of her stature had teenage nephews who were always strapped for cash and could be relied upon to answer the call for a pound or two.

'Ah'll be back in later. Have to move,' she said holding up the mobile to the hairdresser. Once outside she called up the oldest of her sister's boys.

◆◆◆

Rath paid the attendant for the use of the equipment and was directed to a vacant table at the back of the Internet café. He scanned the blurred black and white photos and hoped that Dennison or his crew would have the means to get better definition. He wrote the situation report and scanned it into the combined file then emailed it to Spider in London. In a separate email he informed his partner that he would be staying overnight and would be back in the UK by noon next day.

Back in his hotel room he showered and shaved. A mixture of excitement and anticipation, with exhilaration dominating, filled his being. The butterflies were from the knowledge that he was going to see Siobhan. He found himself smiling inanely in the mirror at the very thought of it. However, apprehension vied with pleasure. He was on dangerous ground. Derry had never been one of his favourite stop overs. Even back in the day, when all he had to worry about was the security forces. Caution and awareness would be his watchwords.

In front of the wardrobe he put on jeans. The thought struck him that he might be blessed and invited to stay the night? Toothbrush! He collected it from the bathroom. Back in the room he sat on the bed to slide on the Capstan boat shoes. The choice of tops was not difficult, it was either the maroon polo shirt – or the maroon polo shirt. Dubious, he sniffed the garment and decided that it would benefit from a splash of Polo Sport.

There was no difficulty in getting a taxi. The cab driver had no objection in taking him into the Bogside but made it clear he would not wait nor would he accept a return call. He would drop his fare on the Lecky Road and that would be it. Rath sighed but told the man he understood. Caution bred survivors and old habits die hard.

The taxi reversed in a three-point turn using the pavement as part of the radius and pulled away with a rapid change of gear. Dusk was deepening and Rath remained motionless but surreptitiously checked out his surroundings. A couple arm-in-arm were walking down the slope towards the pub and two youths sat smoking on a low garden wall two to three hundred yards away. Satisfied Rath walked through the gateway onto the pathway to the flats. He made out the name Callan on the list at the side of the door and pressed the buzzer.

◆◆◆

No sooner had Rath entered the building than one of the youths opened his mobile.

'Auntie, your man has just gone in.'

'Stay with him. Don't go nowhere till I get back to you. Got that? I said—.'

'What's to get? We'll keep tabs. Mind, it'll be more now.'

'Didn't expect different.'

Both calls ended simultaneously.

Before she called The Man, Glenda reviewed what she was going say. MacDermot paid well for information, provided it related to a subject he had asked for. But he could be as venomous as a priest with his sarcasm and had sent many a grown man back to short trousers with nervous urine running down his leg. She dialled.

The connection was made and as it was his wont MacDermot said nothing.

'I've got what you wanted. The Big Fella's whereabouts.'

'And'

'He's there the very now'

'He's very the now where?' The low mocking tone and rasped syllables intimidated Glenda just as she had dreaded.

'He's -he's a – a -at Westlands flats,' she blurted the words in a stammer and hated her timidity.

'He's being watched?'

'Front and back of the building!'

'Keep it that way till I get there.'

◆◆◆

The door to the flat opened and they said nothing as they looked at each other. He had forgotten the effect her long hair, luxuriant waves of russet that framed her face, had on his senses when she wore it down. At the Bogside Inn it had been tightly braided and tied up to the crown. She put out a hand to grasp his wrist and pulled him inside, turning to bring him past as she closed the door. He controlled the urge to embrace her, still unsure, of himself and of her reaction. Siobhan had no such uncertainty. On tip toe she kissed him on the lips and slid a hand around his neck. The touch inflamed him, and he responded with passion until she gently drew away and her palms on his chest, said,

'I've cooked for us. Let's eat first.'

The implied promise made it difficult to let go but, as he told himself, he was a delayed gratification man.

Glass raised to the bottle of Rioja as she poured, he could not take his eyes away from her. She sensed he was looking but was comfortable with it. She was flushed and it suited her. At the kitchen alcove she checked the lamb shanks. His eyes never left her. Laughing she said over her shoulder,

'Are you drooling at the aroma of the lamb or have you in mind something else?'

'I'd be lying if I didn't say both, but I'm wishing for one far more than the other.'

'And so am I Declan, so am I. So, let's eat.'

The awkwardness had faded. Together they cleared the table. Standing at the sink, while she washed and rinsed, he dried the plates and cutlery. He had never been happier.

'Cigarette?' he asked, offering his pack

'That happens afterwards,' she smiled and reached for his hand. She led him to the bed and pulled him down.

He was transported back to the age of thirteen and became that young virginal boy on his first sexual encounter as her fingers tantalisingly searched his body. Each touch intensified the pleasurable, euphoric sensation he first experienced so long ago. Their lips met and they kissed with increasing passion. For him the surge of want was fast becoming uncontrollable. The fire raged in his loins, in his testicles and penis. He held her tightly as if to meld their bodies as one then turned her so that she was under him. Her touch was gossamer light with the pressure increasing slightly as she guided his member into her body. He instantly began to thrust, almost roughly, but she pressed her fingers into his naked shoulder and whispered,

'Slowly.'

She delighted in the effect her body in contact with his created for them both. It had been heavenly that first time so long ago in the German hotel but this time it was even better. His search to find her brought reassurance that this would be a relationship that had possibilities and would last. He was exciting but with a hidden sensitivity and a tantalising but not overpowering sense of danger. The thought of a future together brought a mixture of joy, expectation and a frisson of adventure. The heightened tempo of his pelvis and continued increased pressure of his loins against hers moved her slowly but surely to a blissful orgasm.

They climaxed gloriously in unison.

◆◆◆

On his side he ran his fingers along the smooth hollow between her abdomen and thigh. She shivered involuntarily. He withdrew his hand with a start.

'Don't. Don't stop,' she smiled, 'I like that.'

He smiled in return and rolled over on his back, resting his head on the pillow.

'You've retired.' It wasn't a question but rather a statement.

Realising, after a pause that she meant his involvement in the IRA, he did not answer immediately.

'It's been a long process.' He had begun to doubt his ability to go on, in all good conscience, with the violence that no longer achieved the honourable ends it sought to achieve. For him this would be the first time he had ever spoken of the experience.

'The bombing and its randomness, dealing out death and mutilation for victims, sickened me. More than ever after Helen, my sister died as a result of one.' He stopped and stared at the ceiling. He stretched for his cigarettes, took one, lit it before continuing.

'The big one at Primark's? I got there minutes after it went off. I'd no idea she was there. I was on my way to a briefing.

Firemen and police, ambulances were there. The carnage was worse than anything I had ever witnessed. I can't forget it.'

She said nothing but her eyes were filled with sadness and sympathy as he continued.

'The sight and sounds of those mutilated, limbless beings unfortunate to survive and not die, lying among the shredded flesh of the ones who no longer existed as recognisable humans was unbearable. Mostly women with children, hardly any men, I think, because the majority were shoppers. You couldn't be sure until you had waded through the debris of human remnants.' His voice broke but he carried on.

'The litany of screams, cries and moans was gut-wrenching.' He took a breath. 'On top of the bus shelter there was a torso, the gender recognisable only because it was naked, the clothes blown off and the genitals visible. Vertebrae, rib cages, limbs were littered among shards of glass and the crushed brickwork.' His chest heaved and he took a long shuddering breath. 'There was a small furry toy dog badly singed and a child's patent leather shoe. There was a white ankle sock attached. The smell of burnt flesh and the raw iron odour of blood heavy in the air. I saw police and rescue workers crying as they helped the injured.

'I've tried to forget; I try to forget every day. Can't!' He looked away from her as his eyes filled. Silently she put out her arms and he laid his head on her breast.

Later they showered together and breakfasted with coffee, toast and scrambled egg.

'Do you think we could make it if we decided to live together? No, don't answer straight away,' He rushed the words fearful of a negative reply. 'Think about it. We could live in England. I've got a flat in Croydon and later we could move to something more suitable for a family.'

She laughed but he realised it was not at the suggestion. It was like an acceptance. Almost.

Declan turned in the open doorway, held her by the waist and pulling her upwards so their loins met, kissed her lips. The kiss on the neck caused her to laugh. She felt his arousal and pushed him away playfully.

'You've got a plane to catch, haven't you?' she smiled.

A rueful look appeared on his face, but he couldn't hold it.

'Yeah, I'd better get moving. But you will think about England? It doesn't have to be London. Wherever you want to be is fine by me,'

'Don't be so unsure of yourself,' she chided, 'I'll be there quicker than you think.'

He kissed her again then took to the stairs. He was elated and couldn't believe that she had agreed to come to England to live with him. It was unbelievable. At last, life was beginning to shape up and become normal. He took the next flight down two at a time. At the front door as his hand grasped the handle two shots in quick succession slammed into his skull from behind.

◆◆◆

'Spider, it's Dennison. Look can you get over here?'

'Yes, no problem but I've got to be at Gatwick twelvish to pick up Declan. He's coming in on the morning flight from Aldergrove.'

There was an elongated silence then Dennison coughed and said,

'Yes. Well, alright. See you when you get here. Bye.

◆◆◆

'There's no easy way to say this.' Spider looked up as Dennison walked around to sit on the corner. of his desk. When he entered the office his former commander's demeanour was grim. There was bad news coming down the chute.

'Rath's been shot. Dead, I'm afraid.'

Spider witnessed many deaths, the majority close friends. As a serving soldier and during his service he had, with difficulty, become inured to such losses. Or rather he could control the emotional jolt such fatalities caused. Kennelling the grief afterwards was hard. Somehow this was different. It should not have been, but it undoubtedly was. He could not speak.

'It was in broad daylight. The RUC sent an armed patrol with an Army escort. They'd received the call from the woman he was visiting.'

'Siobhan.' Then as an afterthought he asked, 'Is she alright.' He felt empty, hollow and bereft.

'Yes. Rath took two shots to the back of the head from close range. At present there is nothing further to go on except, I am told, he was dead before he fell. Death would have to be instantaneous.'

'Not much of a consolation, George. Just another fucking death to lay at the door of that madman.'

'We can't be sure it was MacDermot, Spider.'

'No, we can't. But at this stage I'm going to believe it was him. I can't accept that anyone else would kill Rath.'

◆◆◆

In the absence of known relatives Siobhan had made the arrangements for Rath's funeral when his body was released by the RUC. She contacted Spider and told him when and where it would take place. She had decided to have him interred in the City Cemetery near to the flat in Westland Road. She said she understood why Spider wouldn't attend but she did find it difficult to accept.

Chapter Twenty

The P.M. dropped down onto the sofa with an exaggerated explosion of breath. He reached forward for the cigarette box with his left hand then pulled the ashtray toward him with his right. Extracting a king size filter tip, he looked up as Jonathan Powers clicked his lighter and leant forward to light it. Snapping the Zippo shut, his aide sat on a chair at the other side of the small table.

The Premier laid his arm along the back of sofa, crossed one leg over the other and lounged back before saying,

'Well?'

'What do you want an update on first?'

'Where are we on the G8?'

'The preliminary run of the mill negotiations has been completed with most items agreed although there are going to be some roadblocks; the statement on the global warming issue being the main one. The Finance ministers have finished their deliberations. That's the summary of their results.' Powers reached over with the slim folder then dropped it on the surface between them when it was patently obvious the P.M. would not take it.

'The logistics — supplies, accommodation will be a nightmare closely followed by security, our biggest bugbear. Last time, more than ten thousand police alone, were pulled in from all over the U.K. The media lost no time in highlighting regional crime rises with the police diverted from their normal duties and were quick to attribute them to the G8 arrangements. It didn't help when the papers said the terrorist attacks in London were a direct consequence.'

'How's the other thing coming along, over the river in Spooktown? Are they working on it?'

'She accepted the tasking, albeit in her own snooty, cold-fish, supercilious bitch way. I've had nothing back yet but intend to raise the issue immediately after Monday's briefing.'

'Check today. If this isn't going to play, I'll have to come up with something else PDQ. Tell her that we're concerned that this might be another opportunity for terrorists to do their thing. I also need to know where we are media-wise on this so send Alec in on your way out.'

'Will do. Shall I leave that?' Powers asked nodding to the folder.

'Nah, I don't think so. I'll know the contents soon enough when number 11 comes over this afternoon.'

'Yeah, well, good luck with that.'

'Jonathan, before you go, how have they taken the request to use the Queen Mum's pad 'oop north' as a side room for the leaders to have face to face talks?'

'Surprisingly well for Clarence House, at least after she found out about the idea. She's all for it and wants to play hostess herself.'

'Do we need a special arrangement for the to and fro ins. How's the road network up there?'

'Doesn't come into it we'll be using helicopters to ferry everyone in and out from the main venue in Inverness.'

'Nice one. Send Alec in, will you.'

Chapter Twenty-One

William J.S. Tallon, the Page of the Backstairs in the household of the Queen Mother, primped the carnation in his lapel then gave his back-combed hair a final caress with a silver backed brush. He made a moue of mild annoyance as he detected a fleck of dandruff on his shoulder and carefully removed the offending dead skin. Turning from the mirror to give a final proprietary look around the bedroom, he sighed contentedly.

He settled into the high-backed armchair and crossed his legs, revealing precisely three inches of black silk stocking above the handmade glossy patent leather Italian pumps. A glance at the Tag Heuer revealed that his date for the evening, a fresh cheeked Guardsman, from the Irish Guards, with intriguingly rough edges and a posterior to die for, would be knocking on the door of the Gatehouse lodge very shortly. Billy, as he preferred to be known, fell into a reverie.

Although forty years had passed, it seemed only yesterday that one of his many letters to the Palace from his home in Coventry asking to be considered for service in the Royal Household finally brought a result. At the age of fifteen and granted an interview, he travelled to London by train, then out to Windsor Castle. He satisfied his prospective supervisor with his answers and thus began his working life in the service of the Royals. He spent many years in the lower staff echelons at Windsor Castle before relocating to the established ranks of the Buckingham Palace crew. When the King died, he served the Queen Mother at Clarence House.

Now, more years than he cared to remember had evaporated in a glorious twinkling as he rose to senior-ranking below-stairs servant in the employ of Her Majesty. Despite its lowly sounding title, the Page of the Backstairs was *the* position of controlling influence, made more potent by the nature of his relationship with the Queen Mother, which both nurtured over the years. Conscious of his sexual predilections from day one she showed her indifference with a witty reminder to him that there could be room for one Queen only in Clarence House and he was not first in line. Thus, with the confidence that the clout of such a post gave him, he overlooked, secretly revelled in, the snide double meaning associated with his nickname Backstairs Billy.

Like many of the male staff, employed by the Queen Mother, he was homosexual and openly so, even in those years when the proclivity was considered a crime. However, in Billy's opinion, he was not in 'the robust in your face' manner of today's gays. Their employer preferred the 'selfless' dedication and availability unmarried, unattached retainers devoted to her service.

All the below-stairs household agreed that Billy inclined toward generosity, although he displayed a waspish front at times. This open-handedness, a well-known fact amongst the pecuniary challenged lower rank members of the Guards regiments ensured Billy never lacked partners.

Her Majesty's Brigade of Guards possessed a long history in male-on-male prostitution. Perpetually short of cash, beer, and leisure occupations, they stood about in the various pubs they frequented, beside the untouched meagre half-pint they could afford. The Guardsmen, generally taller than Billy liked, were young, normal, and working-class, and if grubby, a bath was a shared pleasure. A bonus was that the majority who rented out their bodies were heterosexual and when he engaged with one of those, on the young soldier's first or second outing, an extra frisson of sheer delight added to the moment for Billy.

The knock on his front door pulled him from his abstraction. Taking his overcoat from the hangar in the short hallway, he glanced briefly at his reflection in the full-length mirror, blew a smiling kiss at his reflection, and stepped out to join his date.

◆◆◆

The taxi pulled up at *The Doghouse* and Billy removed his hand from the young guardsman's groin.

'Eight pounds, Sir,' the driver said over his shoulder as the interior light came on.

Billy moved forward on the seat and passed over a ten-pound note.

'Keep the change.'

Both men got out and Billy cast a critical eye over the other's appearance, taking in the frayed cuffs on the shirt and the stain on the regimental tie.

Thank goodness it's your physical attributes I'm interested in and not your sartorial elegance, pumpkin, thought Billy as he steered the younger man by the elbow into the Pub.

Once inside, he placed a twenty-pound note in the Guardsman's hand saying, 'I'll have a double G and T. Ice and lemon. I'll be over at that table by the big mirror.' With the drinks on the table and the youth in place beside him, Billy looked around the bar and nodded to various guests he recognised.

He did not notice that his young friend also scanned the faces of the bar's clientele.

❖❖❖

Three days previously Guardsman Doherty, originally from Newry, met his brother Gerry, who worked as a barman in Kilburn. After the usual pleasantries, he asked if the younger man fancied making some extra cash and at the same time performing a service for a family friend. He agreed to help, and they decided to meet at the Hawley Arms in Camden.

Doherty, in uniform because of duty at the barracks that evening, soon spotted his brother sitting with a man who looked vaguely familiar but whom he couldn't place. His brother saw him and stood up, although the other remained seated. Gerry came around the table, grasped his shoulder in silent welcome and then walked to the bar to buy him a drink. He nodded to the other man. He received a reflective stare in return but couldn't be sure if the man smiled or not. Uncomfortably, he waited for his brother to get back with the Guinness. Gerry placed the drink before him, lifted his own and said 'Slainte' to both. Only the younger brother returned the toast.

'You on duty tonight? The uniform and that.'

'Aye, but nothing requiring the normal bulled-up gear. I'm on fetch and carry for the guys on the main gate, getting tea, sandwiches, running errands for the sergeant and the like.'

Doherty saw his brother's companion didn't appear to be listening and if he was, showed no interest in the conversation.

'Paul,' said Gerry, 'This is Liam MacDermot. Uncle Brendan and him were school mates.' Doherty swallowed a mouthful of the stout then looked at Liam.

'He's got a proposition for you,'

Liam leaned forward towards Doherty, fixing the soldier with a pale steady gaze.

'Short and simple, this is about a man who chases after young soldiers like yourself. I need to know what he's likely to be doing for the next few weeks, his daily schedule, so to speak. Gerry says that you've experienced what is expected with this type of weirdo. I'm willing to pay well for the information, provided of course it is genuine and I can rely on it.'

'What kind of money are you talking?'

'Five hundred for the actual information and extra for expenses in setting him up. A lot depends how soon you can get started. It shouldn't be too difficult since he's continually on the prowl and a good-looking young fella like yourself would be right up his street. One point that is important: I don't want him rolled, robbed or anything like that and I don't want him to have the slightest clue afterwards that he has been set up for the information.'

'Who's the mark?'

'William Tallon. Works at Clarence House.'

'He's the butler there?' asked Doherty.

'More or less. Do you know him?'

'I know of him, but we've never met. Some of the guys mentioned him.'

'And?'

'From what I've heard it shouldn't be a problem.'

'Getting close to him will not be the difficult part but the information in sufficient detail might be. I want it so precise that I will be sure of where he is at any time during the next four weeks.' Liam took out his wallet and extracted a fifty-pound note.

'Consider that your initial expenses.' With that he strolled to the bar and returned with three double Kilbeggan's.

'It's not going to be easy asking him about his life then remembering all the dates and shite like that,' Gerry said to no one in particular.

'For feck's sake, I hope you're brighter than he is,' snapped Liam at the younger Doherty. 'You've got to be looking for work schedules, calendars, and stuff like that. Diary, even.'

'Yeah, I knew that,' bluffed the young guardsman, glad of the pointer.

◆◆◆

As surmised, the pickup turned out to be child's play and almost laughable in the ease with which it transpired. Doherty moved in behind the older man at the bar of *The Blind Beggar* and, despite the space in front of the bar being relatively free of customers, leant over Billy, ensuring that his front fitted closely into the other's buttocks and back, as he stretched for a beermat from the counter top.

'Oh, sorry,' he smiled when Billy looked up. He held Billy's eyes and saw recognition of the ploy dawn on the other's face. Doherty walked across the floor to an empty table, sat down, and gazed steadfastly at the tabletop as Billy made up his mind and came to join him.

The two made idle chatter and exchanged inanities, Doherty making it more than plain that he'd be available for whatever Billy wanted. From what he had learned about homosexual interludes, Doherty guessed he would have only two, three at most, opportunities to earn his five hundred pounds. These assignations rarely developed into long term relationships.

He would have to go home with Billy and seek out work schedules or anything else indicating where the man would be in the immediate and near future. To this end he suggested intercourse to Billy, who took it as a compliment that he'd been propositioned, before *he* solicited Doherty.

The soldier was therefore totally unprepared for Billy's refusal to 'consummate' their relationship that evening but recovered when Tallon took a Moroccan red leather diary from his pocket, opened it and, miniature gold propelling pencil in hand, suggested the following evening. The use of the diary raised Doherty's hopes, giving him an indication of where he might find the information he needed, and he determined to gain access to it.

◆◆◆

Doherty idly looked down at the back of the bouffant hair, surprising dull and lifeless, bobbing up and down in his lap. A realist, although he considered himself to be totally, and indisputably, heterosexual, he accepted that he could tolerate this if need be; in prison, or monastery, on board ship or wherever else it occurred. It certainly didn't rank as the worst thing to happen to him. *Wonder if this goes on, on the oil rigs? Nah, with their money they'd all be straight.* Normally, suspenders on a pair of shapely legs added an extra tingle for him but on a pair of middle-aged, flabby male calves holding up short black silk socks the magic just didn't materialise. He forced down a chuckle.

His eyes travelled round the room and he located the diary on the dresser, together with Billy's watch, loose change and money clip. *First time I've seen one of those in real life. He's not a Yank, so why?* A muffled slurping as Billy paused for breath interrupted his thoughts. He lifted his head and pulled back to look at his handiwork then gave a wet, sickly smile up at Doherty, before resuming.

Doherty eased himself slowly and carefully from under the silk sheet and sat up. The need for silence didn't appear necessary as the older man, his head half covered by his pillow, snored genteelly. Nevertheless, it wouldn't do to screw up at this stage of the game.

The soldier crossed to the desk, took a notepad and returned to the dresser where he took the diary and the golden pencil. He checked the sleeping figure once before going into the bathroom, carefully closing and locking the door before switching on the light, and then sitting on the toilet.

The amount of detail in such a small diary amazed him. Easily readable because of the neatness of stroke and exactitude of spacing the minute script presented no difficulty. *I'll be doing this all night,* he thought but he daren't miss anything out. *Wouldn't do to get on the wrong side of that MacDermot.*

Forty minutes later Doherty switched off the bathroom light and opened the door to the bedroom. He returned the diary to the dresser with the pencil and placed his copy in his jacket pocket. As he slid into bed to lay back against the pillows, he wondered why Liam would want the sort of data he had copied.

Paid by Billy for the rest of the day, a Saturday, both were free and would go out that evening. They agreed to The Dog before coming back for him to fulfil the rest of his 'contract' for Billy. Once again, the question of the intended purpose of the information he had copied came to mind. He concluded it was beyond him and stopped considering the matter. Casually he removed the groping fingers of the still-sleeping Billy from his testicles and sank into a dreamless sleep.

◆◆◆

Billy was on-duty that night as the Queen Mother hosted a small soiree for relatives of the dead King who had flown in from Germany. They would meet up later. Docherty decided to sink a few in the Fox and Hounds and enjoy several hours of unashamed heterosexual company with members of his platoon.

'Any success?'

The voice from behind him, and its proximity to his ear, surprised him, causing him to start violently and urinate on his hand as he jerked away.

'Jesus, man, what the feck....'

'Calm down. Did you get my stuff?' Liam asked as he fronted the urinal next to Doherty.

'I can't piss now! Feck!'

'Doherty, son, do not, just feckin' do not, make me ask you again!'

Both men finished and zipped up.

'Yeah, I've got it. Gimme me a minute,' said Doherty, washing his hands. Liam did not but stood with his hand outstretched to take the folded sheets of paper.

Doherty waited, surprised how nervous he was, as Liam read the data, several times, then finally whispered to himself, 'Result.'

They left the conveniences separately, both satisfied in their own way.

Doherty, in pocket to the tune of four hundred and fifty pounds, thanks to the schedule he handed over, felt sorry for the poor deluded twat of a homo he serviced. But not overly so.

Of course, he wouldn't drop the dupe immediately, certainly not this evening when several hours of drinking lay ahead, but unless more money, substantially more money, appeared in the offing, he planned to get himself a woman later that night.

Liam leaved through the four pages of scrawled but legible notes and was positive he had the essential key for his plan. Now with Billy Talon's whereabouts for the next thirty or so days defined, his intended target's location would be the same. And the G8! Fuck, bonus in spades! And with the possibility of the favourite grandson there too?

Yes, knowing where Elizabeth Angela Marguerite Bowes-Lyon would be, gave him all the assurance he needed.

Chapter Twenty-Two

There had been no success in locating the elusive Man from Armagh. He did not follow any pattern of recognisable behaviour. Dennison had said there had been no sightings or intelligence from MI5's agents, which was unusual even with the most accomplished hide and seek merchants in the nefarious milieu of terrorism. Nevertheless, in what was close to desperation, Spider was casting his net on a wider basis. Dennison was sympathetic and for once did not scrupulously adhere to the hands-off directive of the D.G. He suggested that Spider might want to get in touch with someone they had both befriended while working with the French Airborne when they had been in service.

Kinnell, on cessation of his tour of duty with the Legion had signed on with the Irish Army and immediately opted to undergo selection, training and eventual membership of the Irish Army Ranger Wing. He was seconded to Eire's Intelligence Service and was now working undercover in the UK. His presence was known to and officially cleared by MI5 on the quid pro quo basis both organisations maintained. The aim of the collaboration was to identify and track subversives and/or criminals whose intentions were opposed to the aims of both Governments. Kinnell operated within the large community of Irish expatriates in Kilburn. He agreed to meet up with Spider but suggested a locale up West to lessen the risk of undue interest from his countrymen.

Aware that the Irishman was operating on a covert basis Spider was surprised to see him dressed in a tailored suit enjoying a large glass of white wine at Geronimo's bar. The Irishman recognised him at once and came forward with an outstretched hand. Spider ordered a Peroni and they were chatting for a few minutes before, to Spider's surprise, a waitress said their table was ready.

'Thought we could eat while we catch up. You don't mind?' Spider shrugged and followed the waitress and his host to the table.

'Though he didn't mention anything specific George said you have an impasse on what you are involved in, which is —?'

'We're checking …sorry, I'm checking on a threat from across the water and it's going nowhere fast. I don't know specifically what the target is or when the action will take place. I think, but am not certain, who is going to do it but to compound it all, I have very little intel on the 'who'. Just a bogeyman. The Man from Armagh. More like a will o' the wisp.'

Kinnell was lighting a cheroot when he looked up quickly.

'He's no ghost. You do know there *is* such a person?'

'It's getting to be that way. I've got a name. Liam MacDermot? Is he of any interest to you?'

'He is. And he's lethal. He's bloody elusive and despite what he's done, his expertise includes explosions made to order, he doesn't leave a trace worth a toss.'

'He killed a very good friend of mine. Don't ask me how I know because I would have to say I can't prove it. But I'm convinced.'

Kinnell nodded but didn't comment. He placed the cigar on the ashtray and spread his napkin on his lap as the waitress delivered their starters.

'I might have the end of a thread worth pulling. I was sitting in a caff in Kilburn, one of those places so crowded that you are literally rubbing shoulders with the person next to you and there were some sprogs from the Guards nearby. One was telling the others about a roommate scoring big time with one of the Queen Mother's queens. Apparently, the guy trousered a cool few ton but the bulk of it didn't come from the gay guy but from someone else who wanted the employee's schedule for the next month or two.'

At Spider's raised eyebrows Kinnell said,

'I'm surmising he was really interested in the Queen Mother's whereabouts.

'Anyway, for a fiver and pretending to be gay myself, I got the name of the young gigolo. He was quite open about what he had done although he did say the guy was scary. His brother who put them in touch with each other told him the man was a Volunteer.'

'IRA?' Kinnell nodded then continued.

'He was prematurely grey, was from the North, and well built. I met up with the bro and he says the name was MacDermot. That did it for me because we suspect he could tell us about a hostage situation resulting in the death of a soldier and a Garda.in Eire. I passed back what I had to Dublin and had a fifty-fifty back from them saying that it is likely the man in question was the button man on the Mullaghmore explosion back in '79. The one that got away. Needless, to say he progressed to other things in the same nasty vein. And grew up to become—'

'The Man from Armagh,' finished Spider.

◆◆◆

He could see the whole stretch of Gladstone Park Road from the BMW. Spider looked again at the grainy picture reputed to be of Liam MacDermot. For one who was universally accepted as being up there among the deadliest operatives of the opposition, the intel available on him was woefully inadequate. The information they had consisted of folklore, myth and fables.

He took another glance at the man with the backpack leaving the building and crossing the street. Check out his pad or follow the man? He could take this opportunity to search the house in the absence of the occupant or he could follow the man he thought was MacDermot. If he opted for the house, he could confirm the identity and then be sure that the action he was going to take was righteous. Despite his threat to take revenge on MacDermot it would only be conscionable if he was the man he observed. He wanted to be sure that he had the right man in his sights with MacDermot having no knowledge of his presence. By checking the house and confirming the identity the place could be put under surveillance until MacDermot came back.

    He made up his mind and climbed out of the BMW and headed toward the two up two down that the backpacker had just left.

    All the doors to the houses had name plates or door mats — except one where the man had just exited. Checking the street then, to ensure he elicited no suspicion from anyone watching, he pretended to check the front of the house against items on his millboard. He rang the doorbell. As there was no reply, as he anticipated, he tried the door. It opened to his surprise. He had expected to have to 'work' the lock. Opening it wider and he stepped into the hallway. In the living room the furniture was cheap Formica and paint chipped tubing. MacDermot had wasted little effort on domestic cleanliness. The place was filthy. Remnants, and empty containers, of several readymade meals. were scattered on the plastic table top. It appeared that the occupant had used a different part of the table, to eat rather than clear away and trash the dirty tin foil holders and plastic cutlery.

In the kitchen. he checked the small refrigerator in an alcove. Two inches of sour milk in a carton and another partly eaten ready meal of indeterminate age were on the top shelf. An empty Tupperware box in the non-functioning freezer compartment caught his attention. With the lid off, he sniffed at the interior then pulled his forefinger through the transparent sheen of grease on the bottom. Gun oil. He pulled the fridge away from the wall. Result – zero.

Upstairs Spider tossed the bed but found nothing. He threw the stained duvet and the broken back mattress to the floor. The dilapidated wardrobe contained two wire hangers and no clothes but one stiffened sock. A chest of drawers, with six drawers each lined with newspaper, was empty.

Fuck! It was patently apparent that he had chosen wrongly in preferring to check out MacDermot's accommodation as opposed to following the man. Spider swore and kicked himself mentally. MacDermot was unlikely to be coming back.

Only the wastepaper basket was left.

He picked out the discarded newspaper and cleared a space on the table where he spread the broadsheet. He quickly established there were no annotations. So, nothing to go on there. He emptied the rest of the basket's contents onto the paper and sifted through detritus. A slim oblong transparent plastic case caught his eye. As he pulled it out, he noticed another. After a cursory glance, he put both in his pocket to examine back in the office. He hurried back to the BMW and drove along the street in the direction that MacDermot had taken. He might be able to catch up with the IRA man before the street joined the main thoroughfare.

He didn't.

◆◆◆

Rutledge stood in the open doorway to Dennison's office and coughed. His chief looked up from his desk.

'Yeah?'

'They've made a positive ID of the burnt body in Belfast. One of our persons of interest. It's Sean Diffin, the Provisional's Chief of Staff. The DNA results are conclusive.'

'OK, Rutledge. Thanks.' Dennison returned his attention to his paperwork but looked up as his subordinate remained in the doorway.

'I can't be sure at this stage, but my guess is that he's our Noone'. He's been rumbled and murdered. Noone contacted us. On a burner as usual. He said Liam MacDermot is going to be the spoiler. Then the murder happens.'

Dennison stared at him reflectively. Rutledge's intuition, despite his youth and inexperience, had been on the money on two previous occasions.

'Give it to Webb. He'll need to get over there to give Diffin's place and possessions the once over. Don't forget we're still in hands-off mode. So, no official assistance.'

'Yes, sir.'

◆◆◆

Spider made up his mind to go two handed to Belfast. He contacted Kinnell and asked if he could break loose and help him to further his inquiries on the subject, they had last spoken about. Kinnell agreed. On informing Dennison of their proposed action, he recommended that they start by contacting Diffin's only relative; the dead man's daughter, as a first step in their investigation. He gave Spider her address in Falls area of Belfast.

Spider leaned forward and put the tea cup on the placemat on the coffee table.

'We appreciate you seeing us Ms Moran. We're sorry for your loss.'

'Thank you.' She did not look at Webb but watched Kinnell standing by the window.

'We understand this is difficult, but I'm sure you're now aware how your father died in brutal circumstances. We're over here helping to find out who did this.'

She nodded silently.

'I also think your Dad's death may be connected to a friend of mine, a close friend, who was also murdered. Possibly by the same killer?'

'Was your friend from over here?'

'He was. Rath, Declan Rath.' He broke off as her eyes widened and her hand flew to her mouth in shock. They sat in silence for a moment.

'He was one of my Dad's younger friends. They worked together.'

'Mrs Moran, I had heard Declan talk of your Dad and how close they were. I think it may have been someone who also worked with them at one time.'

She nodded.

'I'd like to go to your Dad's place and check over his things to see if there is anything to point us in the right direction.'

'There's no doubt in my mind. About who did this.'

Both men looked at her with interest, but she said no more as she moved to the sideboard and removed a small bunch of keys from a drawer.

'The address is number 12 Madrid. Across the river.'

Spider looked at Kinnell who nodded in reply signifying that he knew how to get there.

She pressed the keys into Spider's hand and held it for a moment.

◆◆◆

Spider unlocked the door and stood aside to let Kinnell in. He stepped past Webb in the hall towards the stairs.

'Let's check out the bedroom first.'

The room of the man living alone was Spartan in the extreme. One wooden chair, obviously in use as a night table, and a small bare wooden table across the width of the curtain-less window. An antique pre-World War II suitcase hid under the bed and a battered sideboard, which had seen better days, stood along the far wall. On that wall a religious icon, the head and shoulders of a haloed Christ, hung at eye level.

'This won't take long,' said Kinnell.

He was right. They found a key in a pair of rolled socks, one of three, in the top drawer of the dresser. Diffin's bank book and cheque book had been pushed to the back of the same drawer.

They searched the rest of the house but found nothing more of interest. On the settee in the living room they examined the key which they thought to have significance, if only to Diffin, considering where they found it.

'It's a safety deposit box key,' said Spider. He examined the cheque book. 'Bank of Ireland. Where's the nearest one?'

Kinnell thought for a moment before answering.

'Across the bridge toward town. It's a straight line from here, in Donegal Square.' He took the key. 'We both need to see what's in there.'

◆◆◆

On the plane back to Heathrow they read the hard cover jotters found in Diffin's safety deposit box. It was obvious from what he had written that Sean Diffin had begun keeping a record even as an early member of the IRA. Although chronological, the entries were not diary entries as such but referred to every major action the IRA had conducted since Diffin's recruitment. It soon became clear to Webb, as he read, that Rath's old confidant had not been in favour of all the actions his organisation had instigated. The indiscriminate bombings had sickened him as they had Rath and Diffin compared them in one instance to the mass murder accomplished by carpet bombing from the air. It was clear that he believed in a disciplined approach to action against the Government in London and believed that only in unity would they ever be able to achieve their ends.

Although there was not one case of an individual being named there were several whom Diffin considered to be loose cannons. This became clear towards the end of the journals where one being was perceived as a major threat to the success of the ceasefire and the eventual peace process.

◆◆◆

'More Coffee?'

The two visitors accepted.

Dennison indicated the jotters before him with a nod and continued the discussions.

'Spider, Kinnell good work on this, although if we had had access to it several months ago it would have been of more value. However, that is neither here nor there, now. It's worth to us is that it confirms many of the prognoses we had back then. Its utility for interpreting the future is less clear but we're optimistic. Don't think we are not ungrateful. These have value and we'll continue to analyse the content. We intend to pursue a conclusion to Diffin's murder but that remains our responsibility and you should proceed as tasked. There is one further point. I think it would be well worth concentrating on locating Liam MacDermot to the exclusion of any other lines of inquiry you may have been pursuing. I really do believe that will have results. And Kinnell, there is no objection to this being passed back to Dublin. Thanks for your help.'

Both men watched as Spider and Kinnell left the conference room. Rutledge leaned forward as he spoke to Dennison.

'There's no doubt. Diffin was Noone. The terminology and phraseology used in those books is well-matched and consistent with the recorded calls we have.'

Dennison did not respond verbally but nodded reflectively.

Chapter Twenty-Three

The idea had been Ciarán McCormack's in response to the Brit successes. It was not an original proposition and had been used some years previously in the escapes from Mountjoy prison. However, the credit for expanding the list of ways helicopters could be used was all McCormack's.

The use of helicopters by the British was an integral part of their military strategy against them in all parts of the North. The smaller craft, such as the Apache, were used extensively in the skies over the cities and open countryside for surveillance and the larger types, the Wessex and the Chinooks for example, moved their troops effortlessly cross terrain. They were a consistent threat over South Armagh, enabling surveillance of rural areas and enabling prompt transportation of armed troops to confront any of the IRA's operational personnel in the field. They negated freedom of movement, or at the very least, severely limited daylight passage.

The response was to obtain and use anti-aircraft weaponry against the helicopters. Expedient use of converted barrack room busters, their improvised mortars, had limited success while strenuous efforts were made to get military hardware capable of downing the enemy's aircraft

Less welcome initially was the parallel plan, for the long term, of the Movement having its own helicopter pilots. In answer to the deriders, Ciarán put forward the uses to which trained personnel could be invaluable. The prison break in the South had been accomplished by forcing a pilot to fly the aircraft under duress, with all the risks associated with having a non-willing participant. He described how many individuals in detention world-wide had been rescued from prison rooftops and courtyards, extracted by helicopter, how ops could be performed in tightly guarded environments by launching attacks from the air, how cross border incursions, for offensive insertions or extraction would be facilitated by an airborne facility, how weapon caches could be transported at will. He stressed that it was not necessary for the IRA to have its own helicopters. The difficulty, associated with maintenance would be highly problematic as would hiding the aircraft, but having its own personnel and the ability to hijack one for specific requirements would provide flexibility and be invaluable.

There remained resistance to full hearted support, but the scheme was accepted with reluctance and funding authorised. Liam and two others volunteered and were accepted for flight school and reported to Eglinton Aerodrome.

They trained on the Robinson R22 and then the R44. The requisite number of flying hours to reach proficiency, in total was forty-five hours and presented no problem for Liam although the other two did not complete due to a previously undiscovered hearing defect becoming evident for one and a car accident incapacitating the other.

When McCormack was shot dead his program was quickly shelved by those in authority who had never fully supported the strategy. Not easy for Liam were the sneers and sniggers of other rank and file members, particularly one that suggested his next post would be that of the first and only member of the IRA's Aerial Warfare Wing.

Chapter Twenty-Four

Dennison, surprised to find the door closed this early in the day, smiled. *Open at this time, most days.* He knocked. From a distance came a muffled 'Come'. He grinned.
She's gazing out of that window. Again!
He stepped into the Director General's office. Her eyes remained focused on the view.

'I find this one of the more desirable views of London. Helps me think. The motion of the craft on the river set against the solidity and stillness of the buildings is soothing and reassuring. No distractions.'

He stood behind and to the right. After a glance at the scene outside he turned his attention to her. 'Whereas I —?'

She looked up, puzzled, then smiled.

'No, no of course you're not. What do you have?'

A brilliant strategist and one of the few intellectuals in the higher strata of the service he had admired and respected her for several years. Few of the others were her equal. Tall, lithe, with an athletic comportment, coiffed hair and a sense of fashion she was attractive. Her blue eyes, appearing unfocused at times, were a delight when in a social milieu, and simultaneously, intimidating when questions had to be answered. Pragmatic and resolute she took no prisoners. He determined, on appointment as her deputy, to support her in every way. This did not, in his book nor in hers, mean that he should be sycophantic and accept any and all her views. His value to her he soon realised was to present alternatives to be weighed against her choice of action. She did not take to opposing standpoints, but she did respect sincere overtures, made by the proposer with a belief in their suitability.

Neither sparked a sexual response in the other. Her empathy with the former SAS commander was in his dedication and ability to set events in motion and to see them through to acceptable conclusions.

Dennison said,

'We have had two major setbacks. We may not be back to zero but it's close.'

'Because?'

'Declan Rath was murdered in Londonderry.'

'Murdered? Because of the work they're doing for us?'

'It looks that way. He was there as part of his and Webb's efforts to find whoever is behind the threat to the negotiations. Indications are they were having success and getting close. He was overnighting with a friend when he was shot when leaving her flat.'

'No jealous suitor? No question of her being involved?'

'No to both. We have no doubt it's related to Noone, MacDermot and the talks.'

'You're convinced that Noone's warning of something monumental is designed to destroy any chance of cooperation from the factions in Ulster?'

'More than ever. Logic points to one of the main opponents of the cessations of hostilities being Rath's killer.'

'Webb's partner's death is a high price to pay but as opposed to a setback, it has brought you closer to a result?'

'Yes and no. MacDermot is breaking from the shadows but we don't have his current location. There's a good chance he's here on the mainland but no solid evidence of that. And Webb is causing me concern. I know him well. He gives no outward sign but he's ready to channel his grief. He's seething and thirsting for revenge. I'm apprehensive that he's already planned how he's going to accomplish that. It may not have the result that we expect.'

'By that you fear—?'

'He's capable of extreme violence; it's what he's trained for.' He cleared his throat. 'I'm not sure that the ends you envisage for this operation will be to your liking if he enters the mix with this mindset. We do want MacDermot alive?'

She did not answer. After a pause she said,

'Mrs Thatcher once told me that shoot-to-kill would never be accepted by the public as a recognised policy in the fight against terror. Paradoxically, however, this does not detract from its efficacy. It's a logical response to those who set the levels for violence. There are also advantages. We would not run the risk of hostage-taking to barter for release of terrorists. I may have to re-think 'our hands off until' approach.'
Dennison nodded thoughtfully.

Chapter Twenty-Five

'Last orders, Gentlemen, please.'
Cheatham was not drunk. Seven pints was not enough anymore. Somehow beer no longer had the same effect. He found the room temperature of the drink distasteful. Ice cold Czech lager had replaced any preference he had for warm British beer but the lagers they served over here—here, he reminded himself, just here. He was no longer abroad. He rose and went to the bar.

Slightly unsteady, mellow but not tipsy, he fumbled his key into the lock and opened the front door. The moonlight coming through the opaque glass of the door into the hallway provided enough illumination as he took off his coat and easily found the coat hook. Still in the dimness he moved into the living room, flopped on the couch and used one foot to prise off a shoe then the other. His fingers found the remote on the small table next to him and he clicked on the T.V.

After a moment or two, he sniffed, then again. He sat up. He could smell tobacco. He looked round the room. Then the red tip, centred in the black silhouette of a head and shoulders, glowed as the smoker drew on the cigarette. Cheatham yelped.

◆◆◆

With difficulty Cheatham had made and poured two teas; not voluntarily but at MacDermot's request. He pulled a chair away from the table and sat opposite his nemesis. He said nothing. He didn't trust himself to speak without a tremor as he stared into his mug. He could not believe he had squawked like a frightened duck in the living room.

MacDermot broke the silence.

'I want you to help me Mr Cheatham but before I go into detail, how's the arm?' Swindle winced at the implied threat. He did not answer.

'This time around I'm not going to coerce you but hope you'll help willingly. I need you to do a bit of driving for me.'

Cheatham looked at MacDermot directly for the first time. Despite himself, and he had no desire to be in the Irishman's presence one second longer, he asked,

'Doing what?'

'Driving. Up to Birmingham. I want a vehicle delivered so it can be collected later.'

'And you can't do that yourself?'

'I have to be elsewhere.'

Cheatham took a swallow of the rapidly cooling tea. He couldn't believe he had dared to question this bastard who terrified him just by his presence.

'Why me?'

'You of all people understand why I have few friends?' He gave a twisted grin. 'You and I know each other, and I think I can rely on you. And look, because I need this done, and done reliably, I'll pay, say £500.'

'And if I was to do this, I wouldn't see you again?'

'I'll even give you he money up front,' said MacDermot.

◆◆◆

Cheatham inserted the nozzle into the tank of the rental Nissan and idly watched the meter. MacDermot had been as good as his word and had given him £600 as payment and expenses to drive the vehicle to the Midlands. He handed over the vehicle documentation and keys There was an expensive case in the boot and although Cheatham couldn't be sure it probably contained contraband. He had rejected the thought that it could be a bomb because of where he had to leave the car. He shook the nozzle for the last few drops of gasoline out of habit and crossed the forecourt to pay.

The directions to the airport began to appear as he neared Birmingham. A space had been reserved in the multi-storey parking by MacDermot and Cheatham had no problem finding it on the penultimate floor below the roof. He parked then checked his surroundings before placing the keys well into the exhaust. Checking his watch, he saw he had enough time to eat before catching his train back down south.

◆◆◆

The search through the debris at Birmingham Airport's carpark resulted in the immediate discovery of the rental firms tracking device, as well as the remnants of the registration plates which were relatively easy to re-assemble. Within hours they had identified the individual who had hired the vehicle.

◆◆◆

Cheatham nursed his second pint of the morning. He could see the pub's car park from his vantage point at the window and noticed with only a mild curiosity the arrival of the police car. Two officers entered the bar and after a short conversation with the barman looked in his direction. He sat up as they started to walk towards him.

'Mr Cheatham? Mr Roy Cheatham?'
He nodded.
'We'd like you to come with us, please.'

◆◆◆

Swindle sat on the cell cot with his head in his hands. How the hell had MacDermot got his driving licence? *Rented the bloody car in my name!* Cheatham recollected almost in the same thought that the man never had a problem getting into his place and had probably done it several times. *Bastard!*

He wanted to cry. His interrogators had told him up front, before he had been given the opportunity to speak, that the CCTV cameras at the Airport, and the one at the petrol station, had truly screwed his chances of a believable denial. The fact that he couldn't really give them anything worthwhile on the present whereabouts of MacDermot hadn't helped.

It looked bleak. He could be going away for a long time.

A very long time.

◆◆◆

On his arrival in Perth MacDermot checked in to the B&B in Scone Road and unpacked his holdall. He had left the all-important suitcase in its hiding place in the van. He drove back into the city and after a light meal in Willows Coffee Shop he sat outside in the sun to smoke a cigarette and watch the river while he reviewed his plan of action.

◆◆◆

Liam looked at his reflection in the mirror. He pulled down on the hair on the right side. He had to re-adjust the headband on the baseball cap for it to fit. Removing the head gear, he gathered the hair of the wig into a bunch. It wasn't long enough. He picked up the second hairpiece and put it on. The hair was long enough to form a ponytail of the length that he wanted. He replaced the cap and putting on the dark glasses his disguise was complete.

He stared critically at his changed appearance then pulled up his collar, just a shade, and checked his reflection in profile. He took off the spectacles and wig crossed over to the counter and attracted the attention of the assistant.

'Nice choice. Colour suits you,' she smiled packing the hairpiece with the glasses into a box. She took the proffered money and asked,

'Do you need anything else? Greasepaint, moustache, beard.?'

'I'm fine with this, thanks.' He accepted the receipt and change.

◆◆◆

Parked in the layby of the narrow country road in sight of the thatched roof and path of the house Liam reviewed his plan. After four days and early evenings of staking out the pilot's cottage and his colleague's home, he was satisfied there would be no problem with the initial phase.

The opening pawn would be dealing with the sole occupant of the small house. Fortunately, he was of a similar stature to Liam, neither of them carrying any excess weight, and the difference in their height was so minimal that he was convinced it would not be noticeable to the casual observer. The man's flying overalls would fit, of that he was confident. Fortunately, he drove to the airfield in them so they would present yet another visual assist, in addition to the ponytail hair and baseball cap, that would hinder observers challenging the substitution. His use of Raybans would be additional confirmation.

Important to the deception was the security sticker on the windscreen of the man's Austin Healy. If he timed his approach and arrival at the entrance, giving the guard adequate notice, the car would be able to drive through, albeit slowly, as the bar was raised, without stopping thus lessening the possibility of closer inspection and detection.

Liam remained in his vehicle as the sports car rolled down the gravelled drive and turned left to head into Perth. After waiting for several minutes, he took the holdall, making his way to the rear of the house. There he climbed the apple tree to reach the small window beneath the thatch. The casement window was child's play and he eased through into the bedroom.

◆◆◆

He emptied the contents of the plastic bag onto the table. The empty Cola bottles rolled across the glass top. Gathered up, one by one, he filled them with water in the kitchen and closed the caps on each. Back in the living room he tore off strips from the roll of insulation tape, covered each of the containers completely then taped them, one by one, three each side of the buckle of the canvas belt. Taking the short lengths of blue and red wire he affixed one of each to each bottle. He covered the Swan Vesta empty matchbox and taped the ends of the coloured wires to it.

He crossed to the unmade bed, removed his anorak and placing it over the pillow, lay down. He would wait until the owner's return later that day and put his scheme into action.

He awoke as he heard the crunch of the wheels at the front of the house. Moments later he heard the flow of water and a kettle being placed on the hob. The sound of footsteps on the stairs prompted him to cross to the bathroom and draw the cosh. He waited behind the door and did not move as the householder, whistling tunelessly, unzipped and relieved himself. The man moved to the sink to wash his hands and caught his first glimpse of his 'replacement'.

The full weight of the lead filled leather thudded down onto the nape of the man's neck as first surprise registered in the mirror followed immediately by eye-rolling vacancy. Liam made no attempt to catch him or soften his fall. Stepping over the inert body on his way to the bedroom He took the insulating tape from the holdall. Within minutes he had taped bound the unconscious man's wrists, place a strip of the adhesive material across his eyes and mouth. He hooded the unconscious man's head with one the pillowcases from the bed.

Downstairs Liam pocketed the car keys from the table. In the small utility room, next to the kitchen, he checked the laundry basket without success but found a pair of the bright red overalls in the washing machine still damp. He bundled them into the adjacent tumble dryer and switched it on.

The kettle was still hot. He made a mug of coffee before switching on the TV. Shortly before midnight he removed the overalls and gave them a quick once over with the electric iron.

Upstairs he checked on his victim but as the man did not respond to the sharp kick to his thigh, he closed the bathroom door and went downstairs to continue watching TV.

The chirruping of the birds in the foliage and around the feeders in the garden woke him. He washed at the sink in the kitchen, using a squirt of washing up liquid, and dried himself on a tea-towel before going upstairs to check the still form of the pilot. *Dead or comatose?*

Liam gave an unconcerned shrug.

◆◆◆

Despite the sunshine Liam pulled up the roof of the Austin Healey 100 and fastened the clasps. He put the suitcase on the chromed luggage rack at the rear and strapped it in place. The car, pale cream, was well looked after and started at the first turn of the key. He selected first gear to pull out of the short drive and turn toward the outskirts of the city and headed towards Muirhall Road to pick up Matheson, the duty pilot for the shift.

The surveillance he had carried out on the two men had been relatively problem free. After following Brewton to Matheson's home, he had followed both men in their cars to a local garage where Matheson's vehicle had been left in the repair shop and Brewton had driven to the airfield. They hardly halted at the barrier, which was raised as they rolled up and with a wave from Brewton passed through. Hopefully, this would play the same way on this occasion. Late the previous evening, he had driven out of town to Matheson's detached country home to make sure the car was not back from the garage and that this stage of his plan was still viable.

Liam pulled over to the verge outside the senior pilot's house, climbed out and pretended to busy himself, at the roadside, adjusting the canopy on the Healey. From under the visor of his cap he watched Matheson close his gate then walk towards him. He was obviously not a morning person and grunted a smothered 'Mornin' before ducking to climb into the car. Liam walked around the vehicle, pulling the silenced Walther from his overall pocket, to the passenger side. Matheson was staring blankly, into the distance. Liam fired the pistol across the front of his face within an inch of the bridge of his nose into the bordering field. The loud 'phut' ripped him from his reverie. His head swung round in wide eyed shocked amazement.

'You won't hear that sound next time I use this. Do as you're fuckin' told, *exactly!* Now get out. Take off your coverall.'

At his blank look, Liam pulled Matheson from the car grasping the front of the man's coveralls with one hand.

'Off. Now!'

Obviously shaken the pilot unzipped the overalls and pulled his shoulders out.

'That's enough.' Liam reached inside the car to pull out the holdall. He brought out the prepared belt. 'Put this around your waist and close the clasp.' He slid the hook of the padlock through buckle clicking it shut.

'You understand what you've just put on?' Realisation was patently obvious on the man's face. He had never seen a real suicide belt, but they had been publicised often enough. Everyone knew what one looked like. The weight dragged at his hips.

Liam showed him the small apparatus he held in his free hand.

'This can detonate that from over two hundred yards. I won't hesitate to do so if you fuck about. Clear?' Matheson gulped and nodded.

'Clear?' Liam snarled again. Matheson manged to croak yes.

'Now, get in the driving seat. The airfield! Move!'

In his confused state Matheson got in the passenger's side. He then struggled to get his legs over the gear stick. In his haste to comply the starter motor rasped as he tried to start the already running engine. Liam smashed the butt of the pistol into the shaken man's forearm.

'The airfield, now!'

◆◆◆

Inwardly, Liam breathed a sigh of relief when, as planned, the metal bar rose, and the MG sailed through. They pulled up some yards from the Emergency Air Ambulance reception area and Liam indicated that Matheson should pull over to the parking area where there were three other vehicles.

'So, what's the usual drill?'

'We check in and,' Matheson tried to swallow then continued, 'then one of us signs the on-duty sheet then we do the flight checks.'

'So, both of us are not needed to book-in?'

'Not really, one vouches for the other and collects the weather forecasts and docs then we go to the hangar for—

MacDermot took the 'remote control' from his pocket and made sure the pilot saw the red light as he pressed the button.

'It's live now. If you take the belt off, make sure you tell me. It'll level everything for several hundred yards and there's no need for both of us to go up. Go book in. I'll wait here.'

Minutes later Matheson appeared in the doorway of the building with a folder in his hand. MacDermot released his breath. So far so good. With the Samsonite in his left hand, he said, 'Lead the way. Is the helicopter inside?'

'No, it'll be on standby on the helipad out front.'

'Does the EC 135 have 'George'?'

'Yes. Well, a form of.'

'Has it or bloody hasn't it?'

'It's equipped with a heading and altitude mode allowing hands free.'

Once again, while Matheson entered the hangar, to collect their helmets from the lockers in the pilots' rest room, Liam waited outside. On the pilot's return both walked to the aircraft.

Once aboard, helmeted and gloved, they studied the map as Liam told Matheson the destination coordinates for the flight to Castle Mey. It lay just outside a sixty-minute flight time. Matheson confirmed from the gauges, that they had more than enough fuel as the aircraft's range was more than twice that needed.

'So, no problems with that?' Liam asked.

Matheson responded with an attempted nonchalant shrug but failed as his shoulders were overly tense.

'OK. Get us airborne.'

The noise of the twin engines mounted in a surprisingly low crescendo of latent power as the air ambulance pilot completed his checks and then gently manipulated the collective lever so that the helicopter worked against the pull of gravity until its wheels were feather light against the tarmac. He scanned the gauges once more then increased power while simultaneously applying pressure to the left pedal to counteract the increased torque and keep the yellow Eurocopter's nose in line. It moved higher into a level hover before shuddering as it passed through transitional lift then climbed swiftly over the hangars before heading north towards the Grampians.

Liam poked Matheson in the arm and pointed downwards. The aviator gave a visible sigh of vexation and prepared the 'copter for descent. There was a wide patch of rough grass, home to several weather worn wooden benches and tables, bordering a heathland track. Liam indicated that the engines be shut down. On completion, he told Matheson to get out of the helicopter and climbed down himself. Under the threat of the pistol he made the flyer strip off the coveralls and then throw the discarded garments into the helicopter. He gestured with the pistol forcing the man towards the clump of neighbouring pines where he ordered him to hug a tree before tying his wrists together. He reached around to undo the 'suicide' belt but then thought better of it. If it stayed in place it might make Matheson reluctant to struggle excessively to free himself. He had rejected his first inclination to kill the airman. Within the next forty-five minutes there would be enough mayhem and murder making front page news all over the western world.

◆◆◆

It felt strange, sitting in the pilot's seat where he had a rare, but unmistakeable, fluster of barely controlled panic, as he took the aircraft up. From his elevated position, he cast a final glance at the figure tied to the pine, looked down at the gauges and reassured that all was as it should be turned the 'copter north towards John o' Groats.

Chapter Twenty-Six

    His plan, as with all good plans, was simple but not simplistic. It was straight-forward. He deliberately did not make escape a phase of the operation. He wanted to be alive after the bombing to witness the furore in the Press and to see the negotiations implode. Whether he was incarcerated or free would not matter. In prison, he would at least have care and attention in the process of dying. He knew, in his bones that, although painful, it would not be drawn out.

Liam was oblivious to the beauty of landscape below, purple clad mountains and virid valleys, veined with highways and minor roads and dotted with the dark green of the forests and copses. His headache was raging and the attacks, with their increased ferocity, were more frequent, occurring daily and lasting longer. The sole respite he had was the thought that due to his efforts the filthy maggot of a peace process would be well and truly squelched; destroyed by his efforts to keep the struggle for an unconditional peace and independence alive and well in the North.

◆◆◆

Spider sipped the tea and stared out into the rain. The open plan area of the motorway restaurant was deserted except for a scattering of night travellers. He watched idly as a mother strapped her small child into the baby chair in the family car while an older child held an umbrella over them both. The husband was already seated in the vehicle.

Webb was no longer employed by MI5. The deputy director of MI5 had not been specific in the reason for cessation of his services. There was no need. Spider was aware of the logic behind the ending of the contract. The parting had been amicable and the termination payment generous. Rath had no living family. He contacted Rath's friend in Londonderry and she had given him her bank details for the transfer of his dead partner's share. The conversation had been brief. It was difficult for Spider not to blame the woman for Declan's demise. *If he hadn't visited her, he would still be here.*

Their long friendship had been the reason that Dennison promised to keep him informed of developments in the hunt. The search for MacDermot was no nearer fruition. The explosion at Birmingham Airport was his handiwork. But MacDermot still had more to do. Of that he was convinced; this had not been his main action. It was a decoy action perpetrated to deceive. MacDermot wanted the security services to believe he was in the Midlands and divert attention away from his main target.

'It's still the Queen Mother,' he thought. Which was why he was sitting in this motorway coffee shop on his way north.

It had yet to be determined from analysis whether the bomb had been detonated remotely as opposed to a timed detonation. But he had no doubt. The trigger had been activated by mobile phone. A strong probability existed that the number had been one of the two that he uncovered in Kilburn.

He sipped the tepid tea and pushed the half-eaten sandwich to the middle of the table.

He admitted inwardly that MacDermot was one of the most determined terrorists he had encountered. No, not encountered, he corrected himself. The bastard was so efficient he had only a brief look at his profile and then the man's back as he headed away from the house in Kilburn. There was more chance that he could recognise the Bergen again than make a positive identification of the Man from Armagh.

So, here he was on a wing and a prayer. He had little or no possibility of catching MacDermot so it would have to be the maneater and scapegoat ploy. He had not the faintest idea where the man was, but there was no doubt where the 'goat' would be. So, confident of the identity of MacDermot's target, and the knowledge that the terrorist would have to be in its vicinity to implement his strike, by shooting or planting an explosive device. The Queen Mother, due to the infirmity of age, would not be liable to make appearances in conditions or places where she would be vulnerable. The members of the G8, whom he thought would be of secondary importance in MacDermot's plan, did not count. Consequently, he would disregard them. The action would have to be in the Castle or its environs.

Basic, and almost laughable, his plan was to singlehandedly stake out the approaches to the Castle.

◆◆◆

'Billy, have the tables been set up for lunch?'
'Yes, Ma am.'
'Will they all be attending?'
'With the exception of the PM. He'll be arriving shortly before one. He has had to detour to Aberdeen on his way from London'
'But the rest?'
'Every one of the G8 leaders, Ma am.'
'Good. Make me a D & G. Then invite them all to assemble. When everyone is there, come up, give me the nod and I'll come down.'

At the drinks cabinet Billy poured the Dubonnet and large gin without the need for optics. Practice over the years had long since obviated that protocol.

'Ice and lemon as usual Ma′am?' he asked to give her the pleasure of making her favourite response,

'Do bears —?'.

◆◆◆

Her Majesty's visitors had been introduced to the Queen Mother, who stood supported by two sticks. With Billy's help she eased into the waiting wheelchair. Once seated, he placed her drink in her hand. She refused, with a slight frown and a motion with the glass, the plate he had filled from the barbecue buffet. She entered conversation with the German Chancellor and the PM, who had arrived at Castle Mey only moments earlier and, after a gushing apology, joined them. While the PM was explaining his delayed arrival the steadily increasing clatter of an approaching helicopter halted the dialogue and drew everyone's attention to the sky.

◆◆◆

During the morning it had been difficult to stay awake as he had spent the night sleeping fitfully in the BMW's front seat. As the sun rose higher the warmth increased towards noon. He opened the side window.

From his vantage point the castle was in plain view. There had been activity in the walled grassy enclosure at the side of the building. Servants had set up two long tables, covered with white linen, and arranged several smaller ones around it. A barbecue had been trundled out. He smiled as he saw a chef in full regalia nearby complete with tall hat.

He removed the two plastic containers from the glove compartment. He re-read the text. 'Talk Mobile. My Number xxxx xxxxxx'. Two mobile phones and MacDermot's reputation predicated remote controlled bombs. He believed one had been used in Birmingham. But, which one?

He opened the sunroof then tried to reason which number had been used for the airport bombing; without a result.

◆◆◆

There was increased movement in the enclosure and there were several male figures engaged in conversation. The sight of the wheelchair propelled across the open ground increased his anxiety. If it were to be a shot now was the time. He scanned the surrounding area with emphasis on the higher ground.

He had a flash of doubt about his intentions and the ethical aspect of what he planned to do. Free from commitment to his erstwhile employers his obligation to defend the elderly Royal no longer existed. He would never be able to prevent an attack anyway. He could however, when the assassin revealed himself, zero in and destroy him.

Justice for Rath and his revenge for his death were all that mattered.

◆◆◆

Liam took a deep breath and started a gradual descent. His intended landing spot was a flat stretch of heather covered moor. There was little or no wind, but the wobble caused by his tense over-control of the controls made him flinch and take the helicopter back up. A second attempt was more stable, and the landing smooth. He shut down the motors.

Exiting the helicopter, he opened the clamshell door under the tail boom and climbed into the main cabin to retrieve the Samsonite. Back in the cockpit he double-checked his phone to ensure the detonator number was listed. He selected it and opened the speed dial segment to initiate contact on the one click system. With the side window open he checked it for clearance ensuring the bomb container passed through without hindrance. It did.

Removing the back of the detonator phone he first inserted the sim card and then the battery. He returned the primed phone to its slot in the bomb assembly and closed the suitcase. He placed the case on the co-pilot's seat

In the air and resuming the course for the Castle of Mey the helicopter skimmed across the coastal plane. As the building with its distinctive tower became more defined Liam saw a small group on the grassy area to the right of the main house. He cut the speed. *They must all be there!* He decided that the group and not the house would be his target. He banked into a circular left loop until the aircraft once again was headed in the direction of the castle but zeroing in on the lawn area and the barbecue guests who were soon to be no more.

Reaching across he hefted the case onto his lap. He removed the mobile from the breast pocket of his overalls.

◆◆◆

Spider stared at the two Sim boxes. Which one to choose? He decided. Pressing the digits on his mobile he completed the number and touched the green telephone icon.

◆◆◆

Moments later everyone, except for the Queen Mother, cowered and futilely raised protective forearms. The yellow helicopter, in low level flight, was heading directly for them at an alarming speed. Several hundred yards away, but seeming much closer it instantaneously morphed, changing shape to form a crude eye-searing bloom of incandescent orange flame, framed in an expanding cloud of dense black smoke and a widening penumbra of shards of varying sizes.

She took a mouthful of her fifth aperitif for that day and looked blankly bemused at the cowering Billy.

Chapter Twenty-Seven

In Century House the D.G. looked down at the Thames and Lambeth Bridge. Early evening, the density of traffic and flow of pedestrians below had not yet increased to the level it would later. She thought about the past hour. The meeting with Powers had had ended with a relatively successful result. When he arrived, he requested that her deputy leave the room because what he had to say contained detail of a personal nature.

On opening he had demanded a debrief on the progress of her 'support' for the extended detention period. They had discussed, in depth, the events of the past weeks. Both agreed that this had not been her 'finest hour'. She admitted that she had only activated MI5's in-house team to take over from Webb when, Birmingham airport's bomb attack hogged the national headlines.

She did not address the unexplained mid-air destruction of an Air Charity Scotland medical rescue helicopter. It had garnered scant interest in the national press. Intuition had prompted her, however, to declare a moratorium on the release of relevant detail and to demand that the stated location of the downed helicopter be a minimum of fifty miles to the west. It had ended without the capture and detention of a suspect.

Neither did she share with him the results of analysis of the wreckage that ended the hunt for Liam MacDermot, the Man from Armagh. She instructed Forensics to record the cause of the explosion as uncertain but most likely a technical defect in the fuel system. She thought there were two possible explanations; a home goal but more likely someone other than MacDermot had access to the trigger number. She had a shrewd idea who that might be but saw no fruitful purpose in following that premise to a conclusion.

The PM, Powers said, was 'disappointed' with her management and performance. It had been suggested that this could be grounds for No 10 to request her resignation. He reacted with surprise when she played the surreptitious recording of his initial instructions to her. Blustering, as he was aware of the consequence of its release, he maintained that covert recordings without the knowledge of the person concerned were not legal. With a straight face she told him the recording didn't need to be. Leaks of this nature to the Press were commonplace as he, an inveterate user of off-the-record releases, would be all too aware.

And, after all, she gave a rare smile, the first in his presence, this was MI5, the gatherer of *covert* intelligence.

The End

Thank you for reading this book. If you enjoyed it, and hopefully having got this far, you have, would you please take a moment to leave a review at your favourite retailer? As a bonus I've penned the following two short stories.

Thanks.

Bob Davidson

Bonus Short Story:

Deception

The Warden looked out through the bay window at the wide expanse of woodland park that surrounded Craigie Open Prison. Most of the inmates were in the common room at this time of day. The park was almost deserted. One or two lonely figures could be seen outside, but it was darkening too quickly to be able to identify them.

'Dr Severin is concerned about Cramer. He's convinced that the risk of suicide has increased dramatically,' the Warden said. 'McCreadie, in the next cell, has complained of being disturbed by rambling one-sided conversations during the night. I've also noticed a change in Cramer myself. I don't want to take any chances. A suicide at this time of year could have an adverse effect on the behaviour of the other inmates.'

'We certainly don't need that at any time of year,' said the supervisor of uniformed guards turning from the fireplace. The Warden frowned agreement, returned to the desk, sank wearily into the chair and grunted,

'Just increase the surveillance, Murchison, and maybe we will both have a quiet holiday.'

◆◆◆

Ben Cramer stared pensively at his bloodless hands before raising his gaze to the solitary leaf clinging to the extended finger of the oak branch. It appeared as a small forlorn silhouette against the leaden grey of the sky which, dependent on whether one was optimistic or pessimistic, promised or threatened snow. The minuscule remnant of foliage had survived the ever-shortening days of autumn and Ben was about to wager that it would see out the ravages of winter when, for no apparent reason, the leaf suddenly trembled, loosened its hold and spiralled down onto the surface of the darkened green of the lake.

'Life abandons everything, sooner or later,' Ben sighed. He wondered if the tiny leaf had felt fear and had screamed before it died. Had it possibly died much earlier, remaining on the tree as a fossilized embryo, or did it die when it touched the dank ice-cold water? He knew that death did not always bring fear, or even pain, and that a being could pass over without any great discomfort. The murder four years ago had taught him that much. Two quick deft slashes down the veins of sleeping wrists with an open razor had elicited no more than a murmured groan to signify the soul's silent egress into oblivion.

The gore had spouted in great welters from the gashes to form a pool on the bedside rug. At any other time, he could not endure the sight of blood without gut-wrenching dry vomiting, but he had remained as strangely unmoved that night as though he were an impartial observer rather than a participant.

During the past few weeks, however, the scene had recurred in his thoughts with increasing frequency until it appeared several times a day and, try as he might, he could not subdue it. She was right when she had said that they did not communicate, but he had always found it difficult to discuss their differences impartially when the heat of the hurt was still on him. He tried repeatedly to subdue the anger that flooded through him but could neither stem it nor apologize for his actions until he had given expression to the rage. It was as though he were a cauldron of boiling vitriol, which needed venting, or it would explode, splattering everyone and everything in its vicinity with its corrosive bile.

It didn't help when she demanded to know why he had acted stupidly. Many of the things he did in those days he now knew had been puerile, and he had aggravated the situation by his immature inability to concede.

Ben knew that when he went to the cell she would be there. It seemed as if she never left it nowadays. He could not always see her, but he could feel her presence. When he could see her, she was not as she had been before the murder. He longed to be able to touch her but knew he could not; she was of a different time, a different dimension. The world in which she existed was as restricted and confined as his, and both appeared unreal.

He got to his feet stiffly, turned and limped spectre-like along the grass verge toward the main building, avoiding the gravel walkway. Shuffling noiselessly across the main hall, he wearily climbed the stone stairs to the corridor leading to the cell. Head bowed, he paused and listened briefly at the door, but knew as he did, he would hear nothing. Surprisingly, the cell appeared empty but as he passed through the darkened doorway, his eyes became accustomed to the gloom. He started as he made out the fragile, almost ephemeral, seated figure at the table. He crossed the floor and placed both hands on the back of the chair, but she did not raise her head to acknowledge his presence.

Despite his many rages, despite the violence, he was really shy and sensitive. Ben knew that he was a coward at heart and dreaded mental hurt more than any pain. He did not believe that she could physically hurt him, even if she wanted to. However, she had the capacity to torture his feelings and his well-hidden sensitivity with her moods and sulky demeanour. Those periods, where she could sit granite-still and silent for hours at a time, had never happened prior to the acrimonious days leading up to that ghastly Christmas Eve. Until then, she had been so vivacious, and so compulsively energetic, that he had often smiled at her efforts to do too many things.

Naturally, she blamed him for what had happened to change it all, of that he was ruefully sure, but although he knew he had been wrong time and time again, he could not, even now, accept responsibility for what had happened. Recently, she talked to him more, mostly during the interminable nights, and he would try to answer in a belated but honest attempt to meet her earlier oft-expressed pleas for "communication". It was obvious despite what had happened that she still loved him, although the passion had justifiably cooled. He sensed that she too detested this enforced separation. He had no fear of death or of the mysteries of eternity now. He would not hesitate to do whatever it took to be at one with her.

◆◆◆

"Out on the landing, Cramer!" barked Murchison from the doorway. The two guards ignored his presence and bustled into the cell to search it with the effortless efficiency of constant practice. It lasted less than eight minutes and, as he knew it would, proved fruitless. The search party did not appear to be foiled or frustrated and he guessed they had hoped to find nothing.

"You know what they were looking for?" she asked in a whisper.

"No," he whispered. She rose and went to the sink where she pointed to one of the wall tiles.

"It's behind there." He looked at her quizzically and moved over to stand beside her. When the tile was removed, he remained baffled until he saw the razor blade taped to its interior surface. "It's now or never," she murmured. He nodded acquiescence and took a deep breath.

❖❖❖

"How could this happen," the Warden demanded, "a blasted suicide that we had every opportunity to prevent? I thought you searched her cell?"

"We did, Ma'am," Murchison responded, bowing her head dejectedly, "just minutes before it happened."

"For Heaven's sake, surely the way she butchered her husband gave you some indication of what to look for," the Warden snapped irritably, expecting no reply and receiving none from the chastened woman before her.

"Get the staff back on duty and start a full-scale search before any other inmates decide to 'leave' us!" She turned abruptly from the guard and went to the bay window.

She looked out over the wide expanse of woodland park that surrounded Craigie Open Prison. Most of the inmates would be in the common room at this time of day and the park was almost deserted. One or two lonely figures could be seen outside, but the falling snow made it difficult to identify them. The Warden gazed unseeing through the wraithlike couple, who were walking towards the gate, hand in hand.

Bonus Short Story:

Requited Love

Marie McCracken clutched at the kitchen sink to steady herself against the stab of pain that wrenched her breath away. Mouth open and hunched over in anguish she held her hand against her cracked ribs and futilely willed the torment to subside. She dared scarcely breathe. The ferocity of the pangs did not abate. Then, slowly, agonisingly slowly, they ebbed, diminished but did not end. As she attempted to stand erect and breathe normally, she caught sight of her misshapen, swollen features in the wraith, shrouded in the damp darkness of a Belfast winter and reflected in the kitchen window.

"God h'ull kill me dead one uv these days, so he wull," she thought. The drunken beatings had increased in frequency and ferocity. Even when she feigned unconsciousness on the floor, eyes screwed shut and teeth clamped fast into her lip to stifle her cries, he would continue to kick her upper body until only sheer exhaustion halted him and he would fall, out of breath, into one of the ragged armchairs. Within minutes, his turbulent snores would fill the room and then, and only then, did she risk moving.

Last night had been horrendous. Prone to flare up at any time when he had been drinking, he had come home yesterday livid with anger. The soldiers had stopped and questioned him on his way back from the pub. This was bad enough but what incensed him most was that the patrol had sneered and mocked his attempts to involve them in a fracas.

The whistle of the kettle broke into her thoughts. Protecting her hand with her apron, she poured the boiling water into the teapot. She could hear the murmur of voices behind the closed door of the living room and knew that their meeting was nearly over.

She swilled and emptied the teapot, dropped in three teabags and poured the remaining water over them. The mugs were laid out on the tray. As she stretched painfully to the shelf in the cupboard for the biscuits, she heard the door open and Billy's voice.

"Is that tea reddy yit, wuman?" She turned stiffly and slowly knowing that he would not look at her.

"Ah'm just bringin' ut", she whispered through bruised, engorged lips.

"Aye, well git a move, wull ye's," he growled over his shoulder as he left the kitchen. Marie braced herself against the shaft of pain as she lifted the loaded tray and shuffled towards the living room.

"So that's ut fer tonight. Don't fergit what each of ye's got to do. Musgrave Hospital. Three o'clock. Thursday," said Billy as she came round the door. He broke off as she entered the room. She heard the uneasy movement of the men as one by one they caught sight of her battered face and arms. There was a hurriedly swallowed, "Jesus!" from Paddy Coyne as she placed the tray on the table. The uneasy silence continued until she closed the door behind her.

She returned to the sink and gazed mindlessly into the darkness. After a few minutes the noise of the men preparing to depart brought her back.

"Oh, God no!" she screamed silently as she heard one ask her husband if he was going with them for a "wee half".

"Not agin, sweet Lord, please not agin."

"Ah'll be back efter ten," said Billy to her stiffened back. She did not reply and waited for the sound of the front door closing. As a reassuring silence filled the house, she turned from the sink and limped into the living room.

She lowered herself gingerly into her chair. Almost immediately hot salty tears coursed unhindered down her faded cheeks. After a few moments she wiped her eyes and face with the bottom of her pinny.

"Why does ut have to be like this? Why?" she asked herself without hope. She stared into the comforting warm red coals of the fire.

It had not always been this way. Once they had been lovers and friends; warm hearted, caring lovers and close, inseparable friends. They shared everything, the good times and the bad times. When he had been ill with pneumonia before that Christmas when they were facing eviction, he had been as helpless as a child. Unable to get out of bed, unable to stand much less walk, she was his crutch. He had needed her then and she had revelled in his dependence on her. She needed more than anything to be wanted again. There could be no drudgery in a relationship where they both relied on each other. She raised her eyes to look at the sepia-tinted photograph on the mantelpiece.

He had changed, slowly but inexorably, after that night Seamus Flaherty had come for him, three years ago. He did not come home for two days and then he would say nothing. Almost immediately, he lost his place at the factory and his disappearances became more frequent. She dreaded the arrival on her doorstep of Flaherty. God, how she dreaded the visits. Those were bad times with the riots and beatings and killings. She knew intuitively that Billy had become one of the hard men. He had always sympathised with them. They all did. It was only natural. But he had become totally committed to the Cause.

That's when the drinking increased beyond all reason followed by the fist beatings then the kickings. As a crutch, to keep up her morale she had scrimped and saved almost two hundred pounds from the meagre benefits they received, so that if she ever did find things so bad, she had to leave, she could. She knew she never would, but now she didn't even have that 'out'. He'd found her savings and, well, that was that.

The news last week that Flaherty had been wounded in a failed bomb attack on Montpelier police station had filled her with an unholy but short-lived joy. That same day Billy had taken over the position of the incapacitated Flaherty.

In spite of it all, she still loved him. She couldn't stop. She felt that the violence he showed towards her was born of guilt and unease. Maybe he could not smother the remorse he suffered from the brutality and evil of the things he had had to do for the Cause. If only there was some way that she could help him stop. She felt she was drowning in her own powerlessness. The futility of it all swept over her. She held her face in her bruised hands as she rocked back and forth. Now they were set to go again. Thursday it would be. That much she had heard. When would it ever end? Maybe he wouldn't come back. God, she thought she would die if that happened. But, somehow this cycle of brutality had to end. At least as far as Billy was concerned. When would he come back to her as he used to be?

Only the ticking of the clock broke the silence as she eased herself painfully out of her chair. In the kitchen she felt the teapot and found it still warm. Maybe if something happened to prevent his being of any use to the organisation, she could have her Billy back again. As she filled the cup, she heard the swish of the tyres as the Army's patrol vehicle passed.

She remained motionless, with teapot in hand, her face flushing as the seed of the idea grew. She felt giddy with the enormity of the idea flooding her consciousness. She had the answer. She scuttled into the living room as fast as her aching legs would allow and rummaged through the sideboard drawer for the seldom-used writing pad and envelopes. With a pencil from the mantelpiece, she sat down and, ignoring the pain from her fingers, started to write.

◆◆◆

"Did anyone see who left this?" the inspector asked.

The desk sergeant raised his head from the night register and glanced at the letter.

"Afraid not, sir. It was lying on the desk when I came on duty. I brought it in to you unopened and...."

"Yes, okay," the inspector interrupted. He turned from the desk then paused for a moment. "Get me the Intelligence Officer at Army HQ Lisburn. Put it through to my office."

◆◆◆

Billy stopped in mid-sentence as two uniformed RUC men made their way past the group at the bar. The others at his table followed his stare and turned as the police officers approached. They remained silent and hostile as the two stopped and stood over them. "Sorry about this, Billy," the elder of the pair mocked, "but ye're wanted down at the station. Finish yer beer."

"What's ut about, "Billy scowled.

"Finish your bloody beer and come with us. Now!" the other policeman snarled. They stepped back and watched alertly as Billy stood up.

"Tell Marie," he said over his shoulder to the table as he made his way, between his escorts, to the door.

◆◆◆

"— returned to Westminster from Paris today. Now, for local news." Marie put her hand to her mouth and stood in the doorway to the kitchen as the radio announcer continued. "Here in Belfast it was announced that the Provisional IRA had claimed responsibility for the attack yesterday at Musgrave Hospital where all four men involved were shot dead by the security forces. A police spokesman would not confirm that it was an attempt to rescue suspected IRA member Sean Flaherty who had recently undergone an operation to remove bomb fragments from his left lung following his arrest after a failed bombing attempt. Flaherty, whose condition was stated to be stable, remains in custody. The spokesman also refused to comment on whether there had been a warning of the attack. In Lurgan today ..."

◆◆◆

"I believe we have identified the leak," said McMahon as the Commandant stubbed his cigarette out. There was a brief silence before he looked up.

"Tell me."

"Monday evening, McCracken was taken into custody. Tuesday morning he's out. Bright and sparky. And no bruises."

"How did he do on his debrief?"

A Company commander paused before he replied.

"I've got reservations. He wasn't charged and maintains he was not even interviewed by the police nor was he given a reason for being detained. Just fed, bedded and watered for a night and put back on the street. But, conveniently out of danger's way until the op went down."

"You're not happy?"

"No. Flaherty getting hurt on the Montpelier op could have been bad luck or they could have set it off if somehow, they knew the detonating frequency. Who knows? But, at Musgrave, they were definitely forewarned and consequently prepared. They knew about the attack beforehand, I'm sure of it.

"Who else knew about it?"

"Apart from you and me and the four we lost? Dermot O'Herlihy, but there are no valid grounds to suspect Dermot since two of his brothers were killed there. And before you ask, yes, we did interrogate him—thoroughly. He's solid. That leaves McCracken. His attitude has been worrying of late. It's not that he doesn't want to be involved. Just the contrary, a little too keen for my liking. His drinking has increased but strangely he's able to pay off his tabs at McGinty's and the bookie's. Something doesn't jell."

"I've always respected your intuition, Kevin. And when in doubt, we know which side to err on. We won't take chances.

Take the usual steps for suspected collaboration. Is he here? OK, carry out sentence immediately. Oh, and document these Board findings for the record."

◆◆◆

Billy watched the door nervously. Something was wrong upstairs. This wasn't normal. He had been here for two hours and the others had only made desultory responses when he had spoken to them. He knew they were uneasy, and it seemed as though they were on guard.

He started, as the door opened, and McMahon walked in.

"Billy McCracken."

His stomach lurched as dread filled his throat. He stood. At a nod from McMahon, the two closed in and held his arms.

"You have been found guilty of failing to fulfil the trust placed in you by your commanding officer. In accordance with the authority vested in me by the Army Council, you are to undergo the prescribed punishment forthwith. Take him out."

He could not speak. His legs gave way and he had to be dragged across the room. He raised his eyes to McMahon's stern face in silent plea. A stony stare answered it.

The door to the room across the hall was open. Billy erupted in sheer terror struggling, violently but futilely, to break free, at the horror of the naked iron bedstead and the fourteen-pound sledgehammer leaning against it.

Dermot, jacketless and with his shirtsleeves rolled up, came towards him with the handcuffs and leg irons.

◆◆◆

Marie ran the brush through her greying hair as she stood before the hall mirror. Taking the hairgrip from her teeth, she pinned back a stray lock.

Now that Billy had come home again, and to stay, she felt she had to make the effort to look nice. It was heaven to have him here all the time now. He didn't take her for granted anymore and she knew he needed her more than ever. No more drinking, no more violence. She looked at the kitchen clock. Four. Time to put the kettle on. He'd be knocking on the bedroom floor any second now, wanting his tea.

About the Author

I spent my boyhood on various farms on the east coast of Scotland as the son of an itinerant, and argumentative, farm labourer who could hold a job no longer than a few months. Intoxicated, one Hogmanay, he was arrested, & held overnight in the cells for 'being drunk whilst in charge of a bicycle'. I joined a boxing club to develop a way of avoiding daily beatings. A spin-off benefit of this was winning the Midlands of Scotland Bantam weight championship. In my age group.

I left Caledonia at the age of fifteen, narrowly evading Borstal, to join the British Army where I spent two and a half years in Boys Service and was posted to adult service and on stand-by for the Suez Emergency. Fortunately, that ended, albeit rather ignominiously, and I shipped out to Malaya, at the height of the communist insurgency there. On the completion of three years my next port of call was Belgium, then the UK, where, after selection and training, I served with the airborne forces and passed sometime in the North, Belfast mainly, during The Troubles. Eventually I went to Germany, where I narrowly avoided being court-martialled for punching out a fellow warrant officer who had rather overestimated his pugilistic capabilities. Hong Kong followed the Fatherland where I moonlighted as an extra and stuntman for Shaw Bros and Golden Harvest Film studios. I appeared, albeit briefly, in Bruce Lee and I, episode nine of Hawaii Five O, and a myriad of other features produced purely for consumption by the Chinese cinema goer.

Returning to Europe I was recruited by a head-hunter on behalf of the U.S. Government and after several courses in CONUS served in most of the European countries and Israel & Turkey.

In my free time I managed to obtain two degrees from the University of Maryland and travel extensively on mainland Europe, moonlighting as a tour manager for a holiday firm concentrating on American clientele. With the downsizing of the U.S. presence in the European theatre a friend offered me the job of convoy manager, ferrying humanitarian aid to the beleaguered cities and towns of Bosnia-Herzegovina, under the auspices of UNHCR, during the conflict in the early nineties in the former Yugoslavia.

I retired to the UK and took up golf, wrote The Tuzla Run and have offered my body, piecemeal, to medical science, which is currently in possession of three per cent of it, while I retain the rights to the balance — so far.

Connect with Robert Davidson:

authorbobdavidson.com

Other Books by the Author

The Tuzla Run (2011)

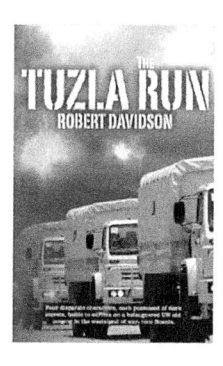

'Davidson's descriptive details of the various geographic areas, and the war damage in the Tuzla region, comes across as personal experience rather than research. Once I started the story, I found it hard not to keep reading the next page and the next and so on, even at the risk of lost sleep.'

Geoff Woodland Australia, Amazon Five-Star Review

The Yukon Illusion (2016)

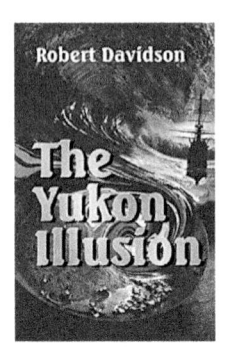

Read reviews on Amazon.com / Amazon.co.uk

Printed in Great Britain
by Amazon